Shillibeer, John

A narrative of the Britons voyage to Pitcairns Island

Shillibeer, John

A narrative of the Britons voyage to Pitcairns Island

Inktank publishing, 2018

www.inktank-publishing.com

ISBN/EAN: 9783747780909

A

NARRATIVE

OF

The Briton's Voyage,

TO

PITCAIRN'S ISLAND.

BY LIEUT. J. SHILLIBEER, R. M.

ILLUSTRATED WITH EIGHTEEN ETCHINGS BY THE AUTHOR,
FROM DRAWINGS ON THE SPOT.

Taunton:

PRINTED FOR THE AUTHOR BY J. W. MARRIOTT,

And Published by LAW and WHITTAKER, Ave Maria Lane, London; and
may be had of all Booksellers in Town and Country.

1817.

TO THE

OFFICERS

OF THE

Corps of Royal Marines,

AND

ROYAL MARINE ARTILLERY,

THIS WORK

IS AS A

SMALL TRIBUTE OF HIS HIGH ESTEEM

MOST RESPECTFULLY DEDICATED,

BY THEIR

MOST OBEDIENT, AND VERY HUMBLE SERVANT,

JOHN SHILLIBEER, LIEUT. R. M.

WALKHAMPTON, March 17, 1817.

PREFACE.

ONE of the most ordinary features of a prefatory address being that of propitiating the public opinion, the writer of the following pages ventures on this part of his task with a persuasion, that in few cases could the liberality of the reader be more required, or perhaps more justified, than on the present occasion.

The motives for committing the following Narrative to the press, were not such as usually actuate adventurers in the paths of Literature. Certainly neither the calculation of interest nor the hope of reputation propelled the author to his undertaking. The too frequently recorded disappointments of those who, uninitiated in the mysteries of the press, presume to look to it for indemnity for their labours, prevent his indulging in a similar delusion, and he is too conscious of his deficiencies, to entertain the most distant hope of distinction by his present humble performance. The motive, then, to be explained, is simply that of complying with the solicitations of many of his friends, the companions of his voyage, who, relying on the fidelity of his observations, wish to preserve a narrative of those events in which their feelings were equally interested with his own. This, mingled with a faint hope that, in some particulars, the circumstances described will not be entirely without interest to the public, have led to the production of this volume. The illustrations will, perhaps, have their best apology in the fact of their having been executed by the author for his amusement, and in their being the first productions of his attempts at graphic delineation. Of the style and phraseology of his work, he is fully sensible how much he stands in need of every indulgent consideration. A life of arduous duty, within the confines of a ship, admits of little opportunity of acquiring either grace of composition or accuracy of language. The writer is perfectly aware how vulnerable he is to criticism on this ground; but there is one consideration which may redeem this humble performance from the obloquy to which it might otherwise be exposed, and this he presents to the reader, in the solemn pledge, that whatever may be the defects of his performance, the want of TRUTH will, in no instance, be found to augment the literary delinquencies of which he may be found guilty.

The Names of Officers belonging to the BRITON, *of 44 Guns and 300 Men.*

Sir T. STAINES, K. C. B.	Captain.
JAMES WILKIE, . .	1st Lieutenant.
J. W. PROWSE, . . .	2d Ditto.
RODNEY SHANNON,	3d Ditto.
C. B. LOUIS, ...	4th Ditto.
JOHN SHILLIBEER, .	1st Lieut. commanding R.M.
H. BENNETT, . . .	2d Ditto.
ALEX. BARR, . . .	Surgeon.
E. TUTTIETT, . . .	Assistant Surgeon.
PETER FORREST, . .	Purser.
——— BLAKE, . . .	Clerk.
THOS. STUART, . . .	Master's Mates.
GEO. LE PINE, . . .	Master's Mates.
—— ROBERTSON, .	Carpenter.
—— ROBINSON, . .	Boatswain.
JOHN BROWN, . . .	Gunner.
Mr. CROZIER, . . .	Midshipmen.
—— WOODTHORPE, .	Midshipmen.
—— SKYRING, . . .	Midshipmen.
—— BROOMAN, . . .	Midshipmen.
—— BLACKMORE, . .	Midshipmen.
—— TYLDEN, ...	Midshipmen.
—— GANETT, ...	Midshipmen.
—— GALINDO, . . .	Midshipmen.
—— SMITH, ...	Midshipmen.
—— RIDOUT, ...	Midshipmen.

A NARRATIVE

OF THE

BRITON'S VOYAGE,

TO

PITCAIRN'S ISLAND.

CHAPTER I.

NOTWITHSTANDING the variety of publications which have at different times appeared on this subject, I feel it is impossible that a voyage to the South Seas can, under any circumstance, be devoid of interest, and as a more than ordinary share has been attached to the one so recently completed by H. M. Frigate *Briton*, I have, at the solicitation of my friends, been induced to submit to the notice of the public, the observations which occured to me during the period of my employment on that service.

B

December 31, 1812.

It was late in the month of December when the Fleet destined for the East Indies and South America had collected at Spithead, and the Commodore availing himself of the first easterly breeze, proceeded without tarrying at St. Helens, into the English Channel. In a few days we had cleared the western promontory of England, and early on the morning of the 25th day from our departure, we made the Island of Madeira. During the two preceding days it had blown with exceeding great violence, nor was the wind abated when the *Fort William* Indiaman became disabled and in want of immediate assistance, which occasioned our separation from the Fleet, and ultimate change of destination. It was two days 'ere we could reach the anchorage of Funchall, when all our mechanics were set to work, and from the most exemplary exertions of Sir Thomas Staines, we were on the eighth day again enabled to put to sea.

At our approach to this anchorage, I was very much pleased with the appearance of the town, as well as with the beauties of the scenery, which, altho' in the depth of winter, bore a very agreeable aspect.

Funchall, the capital of the Island, in latitude 32° 37″ N. and longitude, 16° 15″ W. is situated on the side of a steep mountain, forming a kind of amphitheatre, prettily interspersed with vines and trees of various sorts with which the Island abounds. It is of considerable extent, and rather regularly built, the streets narrow, but from a constant run of water thro' many of them, they are comparatively clean. The inclination of this mountain gives the houses at the upper part of the town, an extensive view, not only of the beach below, but also of the adjacent Islands, known by the name of the *Deserters.*

The rivers running thro' the town, are at some periods of considerable size, and principally supplied from the snow, which, during the greater part of the year, clothes the summits of the mountains, from whence they issue and run with a rapidity, impeded alone by the massive rocks, with which their courses abound, until they discharge themselves into the sea.

The fortifications are but few and of little import, and the troops which occupied them, were part of the English Veteran Battalions.

The town possesses several churches, but none of them are handsome, and with the exception of a massive pair of silver gates in front of one of the altars, there is nothing worthy of notice.

I did not perceive a single painting of any merit in either of them. There is an extensive college for the instruction of youth, in all the branches of literature, and I was given to understand a great many young gentlemen are sent here from Portugal to receive their education. There is a dominican and a benedictine monastery, and to the latter (which is the only thing curious or worthy the notice of a stranger) is attached a small chapel formerly known by the name of the chapel of "All Souls," and had for its motto "*memento mori*," but it is now better known by that of Golgotha, which appellation it has obtained from its being entirely lined with human skulls and bones. Its interior has no other tracery. Of its origin I could only learn, that it was founded by some religious persons, who at their death bequeathed property to a considerable amount, on condition that a certain number of masses should be daily said for the repose of their souls, under the penalty of losing such bequests in case of the slightest neglect; but notwithstanding this precaution, the chapel has not for many years been used for any other purpose than to gratify the curiosity of the traveller, nor could I ascertain that the masses were continued to be said in any other place, altho' the Priests still continue to receive the benefit arising from the estates so bequeathed.

Drawn & Etched by L. [illegible]

The climate is particularly fine, insomuch that Funchall and its vicinity is frequently the resort of invalids, but few, I fear, have sufficient resolution to withstand either the temptation of its natural luxuries, or the hospitality of its Anglo inhabitants, and reap the full benefit of its renovating salubrity.

The invalid can avail himself of a temperature the most suited to his immediate complaint, by being carried up or down the mountain: he is also enabled to enjoy the most delicious fruits, and not only those natural to the Island, but of his own country.

The scenery of this Island is peculiarly romantic—precipices of stupendous height, covered with most delightful foliage, here and there interspersed with huts, and cataracts precipitating from rock to rock in awful grandeur, until meeting from various directions among the trees and cottages at the bottom, they form one general stream, which roars as it pursues its course to the town.

The chapel on the mount, stands in a most beautiful situation, but possesses nothing worthy of notice, except the loveliness of its site, which affords a view as delightful as can possibly be conceived; and altho' the journey to it is tiresome, the stranger will be fully repaid for his labor by making it a visit. The priest who lives adjoining the chapel, I found to be a very intelligent man, and he treated me with great civility.

The inns, whether Portuguese or English, are much below mediocrity, and notwithstanding the little accomodation and abundance of filth, their charges are enormous; and to make the latter still more grievous, the English one pound bank note, was then only current at fourteen shillings.

I was greatly surprised at finding the theatre so good: it is handsome, spacious, and in every respect convenient. It was built a few years ago by subscription, and the most considerable contribution was made by the English merchants residing there, which may in some measure account for its being both in the English style, and equal in beauty to any of our provincial theatres.

About this period one of the most zealous of the English residents proposed the erection of a protestant church, and from the place of amusement having been reared with the rapidity of a meteor, he calculated on a liberal support; but so few persons came forward on this occasion, that the project was relinquished and the few donations returned to the donors. This has been a subject of some mirth to the Portuguese.

Little, independent of wine, is produced in the Island, so that the vine is every where cultivated with the greatest care. Not a spot however rugged, but is turned to advantage.

There are a great many slaves here, who are treated less cruelly than in most of the Portuguese settlements. They are seldom allowed more clothing than a coarse rag tied round their middle.

On the *Fort William* being in readiness to proceed, we weighed anchor, put again to sea, and after passing thro' the Cape de Verde islands and a voyage of little interest, we arrived at Rio de Janiero.

CHAPTER II.

On the evening of the 20th of March, we intered the harbour of Rio de Janiero, where we found Vice-Admiral Dixon with a small English force. Early next morning the Portuguese flag was saluted, which compliment was acknowledged by a small battery on the island of Cobrus. *

* In one of the dungeons of this island, it is said there is at this moment confined a subject of Great Britain, and that Lord Strangford and Sir Sidney Smith have used every measure to effect his liberation, but to no purpose. The report runs thus;—that about three years prior to the Portuguese court being removed to this place, an English sailor in a state of intoxication happened to be in the streets of Lisbon, when the procession of the Host was passing, and from ignorance did not follow the example of the Portuguese in falling on his knees. A friar endeavoured to enforce it, when the sailor fancying himself attacked, gave battle, and the holy gentleman was soon laid prostrate. Our countryman was overpowered, committed, tried, and condemned; but by the *humanity* at all times so conspicuous in Catholic countries, his sentence of death was commuted for perpetual confinement in a dungeon, and when the court moved from Lisbon, he also was put on board one of their ships, and conveyed to Rio Janiero where he now lingers out a miserable existence. If this story be true, and I have heard it confidently asserted to be so, this unfortunate young man has been for a long series of years, a most melancholy victim to the unrelenting and unparalleled tyranny of a government which owes its very existence to that of his own country!!!

A View of the City of [illegible] Rio de Janeiro

The city of San Sebastian, the capital of the Portuguese dominions in South America, and residence of the Prince Regent, is situated on the south side of an extensive harbour, whose entrance is so exceedingly narrow and well fortified by nature, that with the smallest assistance of art it could be rendered impregnable against any attack from the sea. The fort of Santa Cruz, and a very remarkable mountain, from its shape bearing the name of the Sugar Loaf, form the entrance at the distance of about a mile. There is a bar which runs across, but the water is at all times sufficiently deep to allow the largest ship to pass. Santa Cruz may be considered the principal fortification, and is, with the exception of two small islands commanding the channel, the only one in a tolerable state of defence. At the foot of the sugar loaf mountain, is a battery of considerable extent, but so neglected, like several others along the shore, that it is almost become useless.

The city derives but little protection from its immediate fortifications, and the island of Cobrus, notwithstanding its contiguity, is now but little calculated to render it any.

There are wharfs and stairs for the purpose of landing at, but the most convenient is at the great square, in which the Prince resides. The palace was originally the mansion of a

C

merchant: it is extensive, but has nothing particularly magnificent in its appearance, to indicate its being the royal residence of the illustrious house of Braganza.

At the bottom of this square, is a very good fountain, which is supplied with water from the adjacent mountains, and conveyed some distance by the means of an aqueduct.

The water is not good, and on first using it, causes a swelling accompanied with pain in the abdomen. Ships may be supplied with considerable expedition.

It is almost impossible for a person possessing the least reflection, to pass this spot without being struck by the contrast, which must necessarily present itself to him.—On the one hand, he may contemplate the palace of a voluptuous prince, surrounded by courtiers and wallowing in luxury, on the other, slavery in its most refined and horrible state.

Leaving the square, you enter a street of considerable length and width, in which the custom house, the residence of the British consul, &c. &c. are situated.

The houses are generally well built, some of the streets are good, and all exceedingly filthy. The shops are well supplied with British as well as other wares, and whether the vender be English or Portuguese, he is equally unconsionable in his demand. Most of the streets are designated by the trades which occupy them.—As in Shoe-street, you will find shoe makers; in Tin-street, tin men; in Gold-street, goldsmiths, lapidaries, &c.—Gold-street is the chief attraction, and is generally the resort of strangers, who are anxious to supply themselves with jewellery or precious stones natural to the country: but it is not always they are fortunate enough to succeed in getting them real, for since it has become the royal residence, it has drawn such a host of English, Irish, and Scotch adventurers, and the Portuguese being such apt scholars in knavery, that among them it is ten to one you are offered a piece of paste for a diamond,—among the former it is but seldom otherwise. The Inns, although better than in many places, can boast of no excellence.

This city posseses a considerable number of churches, but they are by no means splendid, and excepting in the Chapel Royal, which is adjoining the palace, I observed nothing worthy of notice. Here may be seen a few good portraits of the Apostles. The altar piece is modern, and contains the full length figures of the prince and family kneeling before the holy virgin.

The theatre and opera are attached also to the palace, but possess no particular elegance. The market is well supplied with every article, and is in so eligible a situation, that with a comparatively small portion of trouble, it might be kept in fine order: but the people are idolaters to filthiness, and not less slaves to it than to superstition.

The laws of this place seem to be very deficient; without money it is impossible to obtain justice, and with it you can prevent its being administered. The murder of a lay-subject is scarcely ever punished; the least insult to the church, most rigorously.

The trade with this port is very considerable, and from various countries. There is a Chinese warehouse of great extent, and at certain periods, articles from China may be procured at a low rate. This establishment is propagating with the greatest assiduity the Tea-plant, and from the progress they have already made, I am authorised in drawing a conclusion of its ultimately being of so great importance to Europe, that instead of China, the Brazils will be the grand mart for this dearly beloved article.

The country for a considerable distance round, is peculiarly beautiful; the mountains high and woody; the vallies perfect gardens; fruits of the most delicious nature are found here in great abundance, and the orange appears to be a never failing tree; the quantity of this fruit I have seen exhibited for sale, in the orange market is astonishing, and on the same tree is often to be seen the blossoms, the fruit in its primitive state, some half ripe, and others fit for use. The pine apple is also here, and in great perfection. In the neighbourhood there are several botanical gardens, chiefly belonging to private individuals. Many plants but rarely to be met with in England, were brought from them in the Briton.

The naval department of the Portuguese is not great, but they had commissioned several sail of the line, and 'ere we left the port five of them with some frigates and corvettes were ready for sea.—Many others of various classes were moored off the Arsenal, which is of some extent, and situated near the Island of Cobrus.

The harbour of Rio de Janeiro is spacious, and was the heat less oppressive, it might be esteemed as one of the most desirable in the the world. There is a breeze from the sea generally about noon, which cools the atmosphere and renders it in some degree bearable.

Notwithstanding the entrance is so narrow, the harbour increases to the width of three or four leagues, in which gulf or basin are numerous small islands, some of them possessing villages, others gentleman's seats only. The water becomes soon shallow, so that at a small distance above the island containing the British Hospital, it is not sufficiently deep for a vessel of any burden to pass: but a great trade is carried on by means of large boats. The whole of those islands are very picturesque.

The district of Braganza situated immediately opposite the city of St. Sebastian, is also very fine, possessing the small town of Braganza and a few villages along the coast. Sir S. Smith has here an estate of considerable extent, which was presented him by the Prince Regent in compliment for the services he had rendered him.

The water-fall at Tajuca is about eleven miles from the city, and is worthy the notice of a traveller. The fall is not perpendicular, but broken by the massive rocks which project, and which add greatly to its beauty. The scenery around it is romantic and wild, and until you come to the very spot, the noise of the water is the only indication of your being near it. It is about sixty feet high. On the left hand of the entrance to this place, is a massive and overhanging rock, supported only by three small stones, and where are deposited the remains of a monk belonging to one of the monasteries at the city, who in his life conceived so great a partiality for this spot, that he requested to be buried there when dead.

A View of TAJUCA WATERFALL

The tomb is oblong, built of bricks, with two steps leading to it,—bearing no inscription, but is covered with the names of those people who have been there. Under this place there is a seat for the accomodation of visitors, and also two niches, but for what purpose they were placed there, I cannot ascertain, altho' they evidently appear to have been intended to receive a Bust, Urn, or something of that nature.

The inhuman and barbarous traffic of slaves, is carried on to the greatest extent it is possible to be imagined, and as the immediate and private revenue of the Crown, would receive a severe shock by the abolition of so unnatural a barter, there can be, I fear, but little hopes of so desirable an object being speedily effected, without the humanity of the European states turning their recommendations into commands, and enforcing compliance, which I am persuaded would be the case were the different legislators but faintly impressed with the horrors that constantly occur at this place, and the barbarity to which those unhappy people are hourly subjected.—The labour let it be ever so laborious, is performed by slaves, and it is seldom there are more than six apportioned to the heaviest burdens. I have frequently seen as few as four groaning under the weight of a pipe of wine, which they have had to remove through the town. Many of those poor creatures are bred to trades, and are sent out daily or weekly by their masters with orders to bring him a certain sum at the expiration of that time, and what they can get over they may consider as their own: but they are always so highly rated, that it is with the greatest difficulty they can raise the sum nominated; and in case of defalcation, it is attributed to a want of exertion or laziness which subjects the unhappy victim to a punishment, for a crime, the master alone has committed.

Nothing can be more common than instances of this nature, and as the following was related to me by a respectable British merchant, I can rely on its veracity :—

"A man" said he "possessing a few slaves may be considered of good property, particularly, if he bought them when young and has brought them up to trades. With a man of this kind I am acquainted, who is as barbarous and remorseless a wretch as can be conceived, he has several slaves and as they have all been taught some trade or other, he sends them forth to earn according to their occupations, certain sums and their food, which must be completed under a penalty (which is seldom remitted even to the most industrious or lucky) of a severe flogging. One of those (continued he) was a barber, and for a considerable period shaved me every morning: he was a quiet man, and of great industry, and, as far as came under my observation, always on the alert for his master's interest. For several days I observed he bore a gloomy and melancholy appearance. I asked him the reason, and was informed he had been unsuccessful, and could not render to his master the sum required; that he had little hopes of being able to raise it, and as little doubt of being punished. I gave him something towards it. When he came again, he informed me, that out of thirteen or fourteen, he alone had escaped the lash; but, if he did not make up the deficiency, his would be of greater severity than had been inflicted on his companions.

As the time approached when he must render to his master an account, he became greatly distressed, and despaired of accomplishing his promise. He went with tears in his eyes, tendered what he had gained, and assured him of having used every means to raise the specific sum, and implored a remission of punishment, or a suspension until the following Monday, which at length was granted him, but not without threats of many additional stripes in case of failure. The time fast approached.

D

when he must return. He was still deficient. He reached the door of his master's house, when, in despair of being forgiven, and dreading the ordeal he had to undergo, he took from his pocket a razor, and with a desperate hand nearly severed his head from his body. I saw him, several days after, lying in this mangled state near the place, where he had perpetrated it. This horrid deed had no other effect on the master, than to increase his severity towards the others, on whom he imposed heavier burthens, to recompense him for the loss he had so recently sustained.

I inquired the cause of so many slaves lying dead in the streets, and was assured, that when they were ill and thought past recovery, they were disowned by their masters, to evade the expenses of a funeral, and thrown out of doors, when their miserable lives were soon brought to as miserable a termination. When any of these bodies are found, (which constantly occurs,) there is a soldier placed over it with a box, nor is the corpse removed from the spot, until a sufficient sum has been left by the passengers to defray the expenses attendant on the interment. I witnessed several instances of this nature during the period we lay in the harbour. The cruelties these unhappy people are subjected to, is more calculated to fill a volume, than to be brought within the narrow compass of so small a work as this; and, I am sorry to say, the Europeans, of whatever nation, instead of setting a humane example to wretches whose hearts had been long callous to every feeling of sensibility, vie with each other in minutely imitating their unfeeling conduct.

On the 28th of March, every thing being ready for sea, we expected to sail with our charge; but some intelligence of importance having been received from the Pacific Ocean, the Fort William was detained, and we, instead of doubling the Cape of Good Hope, were ordered into the colder region of Cape Horn, round which I shall hope to lead the reader early in the next chapter.

CHAPTER III.

All communication with the shore having ceased, we discovered the object of our voyage to the South Sea, to be the United States frigate Essex, which had done considerable injury to our whale-fishery, and was then, according to the best information, refitting in the port of Valparaiso.

From the season being so far advanced, we had every reason to anticipate an inclement and boisterous passage round Cape Horn; but, by the pleasing hope at all times so fondly cherished by British sailors, of gaining glory in so remote a region, the storms were conquered 'ere they came, and in imagination we were already at the entrance of the wished-for port.

The wind from the south-east, which may be almost deemed periodical, had commenced, which greatly prolonged our voyage, insomuch that it was not before the 3d of May we got into 62° 33′ south latitude, when a strong breeze from the pole soon wafted us by the inhospitable shores of Terra del Fuego to the coast of Chili. It will be hardly necessary for me to inform the reader, that in so high a latitude we found the cold excessive, and the weather tempestuous. Thermometer at 23°. During the whole of the 2d, the wind blew with such violence, that we found it impossible to set the smallest sail; and the sea bore a more terrific appearance than I had ever before seen, or wish again to witness. We did not see any ice, nor had we any snow subsequent to passing the coast of Patagonia; but rain in abundance, and, unfortunately, the men were badly supplied with warm clothing, which occasioned in the sick-list a frightful augmentation. As we proceeded to the southward, the common sea-gull became scarce; and before we reached the latitude of the Falkland Islands, they had wholly disappeared, and were succeeded by birds of beauteous plumage, called by navigators "Pigeon de mer." Those increased in number as we approached the pole, and left us again in the Pacific Ocean, when they were replaced by a species considerably larger, and quite black. About the latitude of 43° south, we were joined by some albatrosses of great size, but they did not continue with us long.

We made the land near the island of Chiloe, and, after passing the island of Mocho, and experiencing variable winds, arrived at Valparaiso on the 21st of May, where we found the object of our pursuit a prize to his Majesty's ships, the Phœbe and Cherub, and preparing to sail for England. The Tagus was also there.

Our men, from so long a passage, and being so much exposed, added to the great want of warm clothing, were become very sickly, insomuch that the surgeon's list was increased to 109; but, being abundantly supplied with every species of provision, and the most marked attention being paid to their comfort, it was soon reduced to a comparatively small number. Thermometer from 48° to 59°. Our refit was hastened as much as possible; and on the 10th day from our arrival, after taking on board a number of the Loyalist party, who had been prisoners in Chili, we sailed in company with the Phœbe, her prize, and the Tagus: the two former being bound round Cape Horn, we parted from them off the island of Juan Fernandez, and proceeded, in company with the Tagus, to Callao, the port of Lima, where we arrived in fourteen days, and had ten days' relaxation. During this period, we received frequent visits from the Limanians, who are passionately fond of aquatic excursions, and shew great interest when the object in view is a British man of war. On our part, we made frequent parties to the great city, and to an eminent degree experienced the hospitality of its inhabitants. The ladies being pretty, and possessing a more than ordinary share of interesting vivacity, we were led so imperceptibly to the period of departure, that it had arrived 'ere we could have hoped it had half elapsed. Thermometer from 64° to 68° (on board); on shore at 80°.

I am aware it may be expected I should here give some account of this famous city, and I should do so, had we not returned to it again, when I had a greater opportunity, not only of making personal observations, but of collecting a great many materials necessary for that purpose: I shall therefore crave the indulgence of postponing it for a while, and in the interim I will take a brief view of the ports we touched at along the coast, as well as the Gallipago Islands.

Leaving the anchorage of Callao, (June 26,) and sailing along the coast, which at times presented a pleasing or dreary aspect, according as it became more or less cultivated or inhabited, we arrived at Paita, on the 2d of July; a place of little consequence, although rendered of great historical celebrity, by the unseasonable visit paid it by Lord Anson, during his voyage in 1740, and whose name we found still familiar among several of the families, whose ancestors he so ingeniously (and without ceremony too) unloaded of their cash. Soon after we had anchored, the governor, and a long tatterdemalion retinue, came off to wait upon the captain; and while they are looking at the ship, I will take a peep into the town, which is situated in latitude 5° 16′ S. and in longitude 81° W. under a dry, barren, and sterile cliff, and consists of two or three rows of wretched houses, built of mud and bamboo, principally without roofs, and the most magnificent among them only covered with a thin hollow matting: however, this may with ease be accounted for, as Paita is situated within that latitude on the coast of Peru, where it was never known to rain. The interior parts of the houses present a very miserable appearance; yet, I was assured, the inhabitants were very wealthy. The east end of the church alone was covered, like the houses, with a coarse matting. There are four bells attached to it, and are hung at a little distance on a frame of wood, resembling an English gibbet. The internal part of this sanctuary, as may be supposed, afforded nothing to describe.

On a little eminence to the south of the town, is a small battery, calculated to, and mounting eight long brass pieces of ordnance, which are so badly equipped that I think is probable they would not stand a second discharge. This place is badly supplied with water, nor do I imagine it possible for shipping to procure any quantity adequate to their consumption, without great difficulty. The country for many leagues is barren, and uncultivated. Piura is the nearest town, in whose jurisdiction it is.

In the afternoon, the governor, chief officers, and families, to the number of a score, came off to a dinner, which the captain had prepared for them, when those people, who in the morning appeared in as great a state of destitution as their houses, were clad in the most fantastic and costly attire. Some of them had even been resolute enough to shave themselves. The old priest, who besides his spiritual situation, kept a considerable shop, wishing to make hay while the sun-shone, brought off with him a bale of Guayaquil hats, one of which I bartered for an old pair of silk stockings, being more esteemed than money, but I do not imagine he found a very brisk sale.

The fashion for the ladies to go without pockets, was clearly proved, not to have reached this place, for the captains steward having missed some plate, and fancying he saw one

E

of the ladies in treaty with a silver knife, he took the liberty of requesting to examine hers, where, to her great confusion, some of the articles were found; but it may be urged in extenuation of her fault, that Lord Anson, at his visit there, had played a trick or two on the family, from whom she was descended.

We sailed the same night, still keeping close to the shore, and passing the Islands of Lobus de Mar and Terra, arrived off the river Tumbiz, where we anchored and remained three days, cut a large quantity of wood on an Island in a small creek, a little to the northward of the river: we found some foxes here and took two. There is a bar crossing the entrance of the river Tumbiz, which renders it difficult, and at times, rather dangerous for boats to cross; notwithstanding ships can be supplied with water which is of very good quality. It was on this place a boat belonging to the Phœbe was upset, which occasioned the death of Lieut. Jago, and the Purser, but whether they were drowned or eaten by the Alligators is uncertain. Several of these frightful creatures were seen next morning basking themselves in the sun, and both these gentlemen being good swimmers, one may be led to conclude they reached the shore only to die a more wretched death. This ferocious animal, as it is said by naturalists, continues to grow while it lives, and those I saw were of different sizes, from six to eighteen feet. One of ten feet long was shot. They are of a dark green color, with large and almost impenetrable scales, and, although in opposition to the opinion of many writers who have treated on the subject, I believe of considerable bravery.

The town of Tumbiz, at a small distance from the mouth of the river, is of inconsiderable extent, although of some celebrity in the history of Peru, from its having been one of the last towns subjected by the Incas, and the place where Pizarro and his companions in their first expedition landed.[1] In their second expedition, they again visited Tumbiz, and formed their first settlement St Michael[2] on the river Piura. After Huayna Capac the eleventh Inca, had brought this province under his subjection, which was effected without much opposition, he dedicated a temple to the sun, a most stately and magnificent temple, the remains of which I have been informed, are still visible. At the distance of a few leagues to the north, is the river and town of Guayaquil, where terminate the kingdom of

1 Garcilleso De la Vega, book 9, Chapter 2.

2 Robertsons history of America, book 6, page 125.

Peru; Guayaquil being in the district and Vice-royalty of Quito.

We next visited St. Helena, a place of little importance, and remarkable only for the high point of land, which has every appearance of being an Island, until you are within a small distance of the shore. On a sandy beach to the northward of the point, is a small town, whose inhabitants are chiefly natives of the country. The houses being nothing but frames or skeletons, and having no high land behind them, appear rather extraordinary. The floor on which the people live, is about six or eight feet from the ground, and the ladder by which they ascend, is always drawn up at night, otherwise they would run great risk of being bit by serpents which infest the place, and whose bite is venomous. This reptile is very small, and nearly a yard in length, I saw but one. We took a few fish here, and likewise procured a few boat-load of water.

We now steered to the Island of Plata, which to our great surprise, we found destitute of water, and, although possessed of some wood, it was not to be got at but with so much difficulty, that we left it and proceeded to the Island of Salango, between which and the Main we anchored, where we found both the above articles in great abundance. From the surf being continual and exceedingly violent, it is necessary to land the casks and raft them off to the ship. The water is rather muddy, but soon settles and is very good. There are only two houses here, built similar to those of St. Helena, and are occupied by a family of the natives of the country. In this neighbourhood there are some tigers, and the serpents are of a considerable size as well as venomous.

Having now completed the ships with water, we left the coast of America for the purpose of examining the group of Islands known by the name of the Gallipagos, and on the 25th July, arrived at Charles Island, and anchored in an harbour sufficiently commodious to contain a very considerable force. This Island is perfectly barren, and excepting the prickly peach tree, which grows to an immense size, and a few bushes along the beach, there is no appearance of the least vegetation. There are the craters of several old volcanoes, but I did not perceive the trace of any recent eruption. Guanas we found here in great abundance, and notwithstanding their disgusting appearance, they were eaten by many of the sailors, who esteemed them as most delicious food. We found also a great many small birds resembling, but more diminutive than the wood pigeon. They were so exceedingly tame, that many were taken without the least attempt to escape, and when a stone or stick was thrown, it was seldom they flew away, but remained until struck or killed. This Island is often visited by great quantities of seals. We found but few tortoises and no water. Tarrying here one day, we proceeded to Chatham Island, which excepting a small isthmus, where the volcanoes have not extended their ravages, is a perfect body of black lava. Here we were fortunate in our search for tortoises, and took more than a hundred, among them were several weighing upwards of 370 lbs. Amongst the grass on the isthmus, we took some land tortoise. One of these creatures greatly exceeded the others in size, and as the progress this species make in growing, is particularly slow, I am led to conclude it to have been of a great age. From its having been taken at this Island, the sailors whimsically bestowed on it the name of Lord Chatham. It soon lost its natural shyness, became much petted among the crew, and latterly, was in regular attendance in the galley at the hour of meals, when it partook of the ships allowance, and was fed by the men either out of their hands or some of their utensils, but notwithstanding, every care was taken, its life could not be preserved in the excessive cold, of a high southern latitude.

War
RECEIVED.

The Kicker rock, stands in the center of this anchorage, and has a most extraordinary appearance. In our search for water here as at Charles Island, we were unsuccessful.

At James's Island we found a good anchorage, a considerable quantity of wood, and at the foot of an exceedingly high and remarkable mountain, a small stream of water, near which is the remains of the hut of an unfortunate Spaniard, who was left there by his companions, and where he remained nearly two years. Land tortoises are found here in great abundance, whose meat being very fine, we found it a great relief from salt provisions. The number of guanas we saw here, can alone be conceived; they had regular burrows, and were much more plentiful than I have ever seen rabbits in a preserve in this country. They are of a light red color, about two to three feet long, and when pursued, do not like those at Charles Island, take to the water. Among some green bushes near the beach, is the tomb of Lieut. Cowen, of the United States Frigate, Essex, who fell in a duel with Mr. Gamble of that ship. That this unfortunate young man was much esteemed by his brother officers, is evident from the great respect they paid to his memory. The thermometer in the shade, at 88° on board, and on shore also in the shade, at 95°.

Albermarle Island, the most extensive of this group, is nearly covered by the numerous volcanic eruptions, which appear to have recently taken place. It possesses no fresh water, but the numerous plants and shrubs would, to a botanist, be a source of infinite gratification. Many of those plants, and which are exceedingly beautiful, grow immediately from solid lumps of black lava, not having the least appearance of possessing any thing sufficiently nutritious, or at all calculated to support a shrub in so high a state of vegetation. I removed one on board, and although a very considerable quantity of the lava was taken with it, it died immediately. It had a leaf resembling velvet, and when broken, an abundance of milky juice of a strong astringent nature issued. This plant was very odorous. There are some small birds here, also lizards and grasshoppers, the latter are of great size as well as beauty.

Norborough Island, vies with the others in its dark, gloomy, and mountainous appearance. It is covered with volcanoes, and two were burning when we passed it. This Island does not possess fresh water, or vegetation. There is a very strong and continual current or indraft towards this group, which I suppose supplies the numerous volcanoes, with which they collectively abound.

Our examination of these Islands occupied us ten days, when we again put to sea, and after a short voyage arrived at the more pleasing, as well as interesting, group of the Marquesas.

CHAPTER IV.

We had departed from those gloomy Islands, 'ere we perceived it to be the intention of Sir Thomas Staines to visit the Marquesas; but the course he ordered the ship to be steered, soon demonstrated his object, and on the 14th day, subsequent to our departure from Narborough, we arrived at Novaheevah, or Sir Henry Martyn's Island, having run in that period a distance exceeding 3,000 miles. At our approach to Port Anna Maria, it became almost a calm, when we were met by a boat, apparently European, which proved to have belonged to one of the whalers taken by the United States Frigate Essex, and now in possession of Wilson, a native of England, who having left an English merchant ship about ten years before, remained there ever since. It was necessary to anchor off the entrance for the night, and early next morning, availing ourselves of the sea breeze, we entered this delighful harbour, when we anchored in a small bay, which Captain David Porter, of the United States Navy, had occupied, and on an adjacent mountain had thrown up some works for his protection, of which, in the course of this chapter, I shall have to treat more largely.

We were now informed by Wilson, that our appearance off the Island, had been the occasion of considerable alarm, and that the Natives, (dreading it to be the return of Captain Porter, who, doubtless, would have taken ample vengeance for the fate of those of his men, whom they had stoned to death, in retaliation for the brutal conduct he exemplified towards them, during his stay in the Port;) had deserted the Valley, and were seeking safety by flight; but on finding our ship to be of another nation, they soon returned, and at our approach, the shore was crowded, each waving a branch of the palm tree as a signal of friendship.

As the first boat drew near the shore, about thirty of the natives ran into the water to receive her, which was done with so much dexterity and strength, that she was carried bodily upon the beach, without giving any of the crew sufficient time to quit her. This had a much prettier effect than I can well describe, and I was infinitely more pleased at beholding such a demonstration of friendship, than I possibly could have been at experiencing it.

The Captain now waited on the King in form, who received him with great kindness and made every friendly profer of assistance. His Majesty after having asked how many pigs, bread-fruit, and cocoa nuts we wanted, solicited to know the number of ladies both ships would require, because he was doubtful his valley would be deficient, and in which case, he would send to a neighbouring kingdom for a supply. His politeness was fully appreciated, and I believe, there are few Royal Personages of the present day who would be more accommodating, or give to their friendship a greater latitude.

The first ceremony being over,—a friendship established,—and the intercouse with the natives becoming unrestricted, each successive day was productive of something new; but 'ere I proceed to the relation, it may not be improper for the information of those of my readers who are not adepts in geography, if I take a brief view of the local situation of the Island, which is one of the most considerable, as well as fertile, among the group lying within the Latitude of 8° and 10° south, and in longitude 138° 15' to 140° 25' west, and discovered by Don Alvera Mendana de Neyra, in the year 1595, who named them jointly, the Marquesas, in compliment to Mendoça Marquis de Canete, the then viceroy of Peru, under whose auspices he had been sent out on a voyage of discovery. Subsequent to this period, they have been often visited by ships of different nations, and it has been asserted that Ingraham, an American, was the first who discovered Novaheevah, and from which, I am inclined to suppose, Captain Porter's pompous and ridiculous claim to priority of discovery is founded: but the Islands Ingraham seen, appear to be those mentioned by the French Navigator, Le Merchand, and which are situated at a small distance to the north west of the Marquesas.

Novaheevah, the signification of which I could not ascertain, received from Lieut. Hergest, the name of Sir Henry Martyn's Island, and by which it is now generally known.

This island, as I have already said, is not only more extensive than the others, but also of greater fertility. It is divided into several districts or vallies, each containing from 1500 to 2000 people, with an hereditary King attached to each. These Tribes or Nations are frequently at war with each other, but I believe seldom come to a general battle, and which is as seldom sanguinary; still the mode they pursue, may be productive of greater calamity than the loss of a few slain, for they frequently go by night into a neighbouring district, and destroy the bark from every bread-fruit,* or Cocoa-nut tree they meet with, which

* After the bread-fruit tree has been thus treated, it is five years' ere it will again bear fruit.

being their general food, a ravage of this kind is certain to involve the unfortunate district in want for several subsequent years; insomuch that its inhabitants become dependant on the adjoining villages for subsistence. In the several kingdoms of the Pytees, Haupaws, and Typees, I saw an exceeding number of trees which had undergone this barbarous operation, and from whence many of the inhabitants had not only been obliged to remove, but to solicit the aid of their neighbours.

Port Anna Maria, or the bay of Tuhuouy, forms one of the most considerable districts of which the natives call themselves Pyteès---beyond the mountains are the Haupaws, and those inhabiting the Valley in Comptroller's Bay, are called Typees, who are said to be the most warlike in the Island, as well as being a species of the Anthropophagi, but I am yet to learn, how they gained this unnatural reputation, for when I made an incursion into the interior of their country, I could not perceive the least trace of cannibility among them, or aught, to authorize my drawing so horrible a conclusion. The manners and customs of those tribes, resemble each other in every thing, but, perhaps, those of the valley of Tuhuouy are the most civilized, as it is a Port where ships occasionally touch for the purpose of procuring Sandle wood for the market of Canton.

This place is surrounded by a ridge of mountains of almost inaccessible height, forming the boundary of the kingdom, which is divided and subdivided into villages or districts, each having a chief, tributary to the king, who is at all times ready to lead his warriors to battle at the sound of the conch. Every kingdom has a chief priest, and to each of the divisions a subordinate one, who are much respected, and ever held in the greatest veneration.

Their religion, as well as their mode of performing it, appears to differ but little from the description given in the appendix to the Missionary voyage to the Society Islands, excepting that of offering human sacrifices to their Eatōōa or God. I could not find that this custom had ever been in practice here; if it had, it must have been very ancient, for it did not form any part of their numerous traditionary stories. The Eatōōa appears throughout these Islands, to be the superior deity, but they have many of inferior note, and amongst them I remarked Fatu-aitapōō, and two or three others resembling in sound those mentioned in the Missionary voyage, (page 143) but the one here mentioned, alone corresponded exactly. Every family have also a deity of their own, taken from an illustrious relative whom they suppose has from his virtue, or great actions, become an Eatōōa. To him they dedicate images cut out of wood, and although the figures are uncouthly represented, they are very ingenious. These are sacred, and principally used for the tops of crutches, or stilts, as they are superstitious enough to suppose, that when they rest on these images they will be secure from injury; and if by accident they are unfortunate enough to stumble, it is seldom they live long afterwards; for if the Priest cannot satisfactorily appease the anger of the Tutelar Eatōōa, they fancy they labor under his displeasure, and with an unequalled resignation and calmness starve themselves to death.

In the performance of all ceremonies, they exemplify the greatest devotion, nor do they at any time approach a place sacred to the Eatōōa without the most marked respect. The women uncovering their bosoms, the men removing their hats. Of the evil demon or Vehēēné ihēē they have but little dread, being firmly persuaded that after the soul has taken its departure from the body, it will enjoy a rank among their Eatōōas in another world, according as its life has been good or bad in this. Nothing can exceed their superstition; they are constantly seeing Atōōwās, or Ghosts, and in their sleep, even, they fancy the soul leaves the body to repose among its kindred spirits.

The morais, or burial places at this place, are greatly inferior to what I was led to expect, as from the description of several navigators I anticipated something exceedingly handsome, but they consist merely of a large heap of stones, very irregularly piled, having on the top a small house for the purpose of receiving the remains of the King, his family, or those of the principal Chiefs; the sacrifices are also made here, and from the place being Tabooed, or rendered sacred, the women, who labor under great restriction, are precluded from going to, or even touching it, under the heavy penalty of death. Their regret at the loss of a friend is demonstrated in various ways, and are borne away by the most opposite and sudden gusts of passion, and if a woman be weeping over a dead child (for they are very affectionate) you may expect (as I was informed) her sorrow to be turned into joy, and that she will be laughing with a glee equal to her former grief; but nothing of this nature came immediately under my notice.

Their places of public assembly, are much superior to the morais, and are generally extensive enough within to contain 1000, or 1200 people. This spot is also tabooed, and consequently the ladies, whose interference in any political matter is never allowed, are prohibited

G

visiting it, under the penalty I have before mentioned. The most spacious as well as elegant of these, is in the kingdom of the Typees.

The exchanging names, or becoming a brother with a chief, or native, seems to be a general custom, and indeed there can be no greater advantage to a stranger, for when an adoption of this nature takes place, the chief considers his Tayo, or brother, equally with himself, entitled to what his house, or district affords, and his people pay him the same respect. Patookee, a chief of great celebrity, solicited a Tayoship with me, to which I acceded, when he placed on my head his own hat as a token of friendship. It is of a simple structure, made from the leaf of the palm tree, but I shall ever hold it in the greatest estimation. The benefit I derived from my new connection was incalculable—he was in constant attendance, and seldom came without offering me presents. From this Tayo there is nothing withheld, even the most favorite lady would be ceded with the greatest complacency. The reader will, I doubt not, imagine where female chastity is so little esteemed, and of no recommendation to the sex, there can be but a small portion of the affection of a father, a husband, or a friend. The wife too, he may suppose, is equally callous to every feeling of sensibility:—but I can assure him, an impression of this kind would be very erroneous, for I am firmly persuaded, notwithstanding their readiness to deliver their wives, or daughters, into the embraces of strangers, they possess to an eminent degree the finest feelings of friendship. I have often seen the men fondling and hugging their children with as great appearance of affection, as can well be described, and that the women are impressed with the strongest attachment for their immediate Lords, the circumstance I am about to adduce will be sufficient to prove:—Lieut. Bennet, of the Royal Marines, took for his Tayo a young man of an exceedingly interesting and penetrating countenance, in stature manly, and whose wife also possessed more than ordinary beauty. From the attention shewn him, he conceived a desire to visit England, and was, I believe, promised permission should be granted him. His intention was soon communicated to his wife, who an evening or two after, when we were walking on the beach, came up to us in the most frantic and wild manner, talking with unequalled rapidity, but not a word could we distinguish but "Vahana Picatanee" or husband to England. She cried and laughed alternately, tore her hair—beat her breast—lay down on the ground—danced, sang, and at length in a paroxysm of despair, cut herself in several places with a shark's tooth, which until then she had concealed, nor could we disarm her 'ere she had done herself considerable injury. She was still frantic, and we still ignorant of the cause, and should have remained so, had not Otaheitean Jack * arrived, who informed us, when we assured her, her fears were vain, and that her husband should not be permitted to go from the Island without her leave. This had the desired effect, and she soon became as placid and cheerful as ever; nor did she appear to notice the wounds she had inflicted. There were several spectators to this affecting scene, which clearly proved that the natives of this remote region, although in a perfect state of nature, are neither destitute of feelings nor affection. Old age is no where more respected or revered than here.

I am decidedly of opinion that the custom of having plurality of wives is confined to the chiefs alone, and that the people in general are constant to one, and in this I am supported by the opinion of Crook, the Missionary, who says, speaking of the Island of St. Christina,

* A Native of Otaheite, who had been taught a little English by the Missionaries.

(M. V. page 144) "Observing a pregnant woman I asked her how many children she had? She replied three. I wished to know if they were by the same man? she said yes. I asked farther if he had any other wife? she said no. Whence I am led to believe that though Tenae* has more wives than one, this is not usual, and may be the privilege of the chief." The continuation of this paragraph, tends greatly to strengthen what I have already said, relative to their affection, for says he, "They seem to be very fond of their children, and when I went up to the valley, I saw the men often dandling them upon their knees, exactly as I have observed an old grandfather with us in a country village."

The Nooaheevahans, like most of those of the other Islands, have no regular meals, nor are the women employed in any part of the cookery, except for themselves, and are prohibited from eating at all of the hog, notwithstanding they are very fond of it, for those who came on board ate of it most voraciously. They do not eat much at a time, but their meals are frequent, and their dishes consist chiefly of the bread-fruit roasted, fish, which they eat raw, Ahee-nuts, a root resembling the yam, beat in-

* Chief or King in the Island of Christina, by whom Crook the Missionary was patronized.

to a paste, and roast pork. Poultry they have also, but in no great abundance, nor did they appear to like its meat. These articles are generally served up in calabash, or cocoa-nut shells—their knives are made from the outside of bamboo, and their forks of the same materials, but resembling a wooden skewer. These instruments are seldom used, but for the first separation. It is rarely they employ themselves at work, and excepting a few old men, who were making nets, or canoes, I never saw any.

The clothing, or dress of these people is very simple, the men having nothing but the *ăme* or girdle of cloth round their waist, which is passed between their legs and neatly secured in front. They have also a hat made from the palm tree, the simplicity of which gives an interesting finish to their manly statures. They are excessively fond of ear ornaments, the men making theirs from sea shells, or a light wood, which by the application of an earth, becomes beautifully white. The women prefer flowers, and which at all seasons are to be found. Whales teeth, are held in so much estimation that a good one is considered equal to the greatest property; they are generally in the possession of the Chiefs, who wear them suspended round their neck. Their other species of dress consists of a kind of Coronet, ingeniously made from a light wood, on which is fastened, by means of the rosin from the bread-fruit tree, small red berries; a great quantity of feathers give the finish. The ruff worn round the neck, is made of the same materials, Added to these are large bunches of human hair, tied round the ancles, wrist, or neck, and always worn in battle, though seldom otherwise. Tattooing is evidently considered among them a species of dress, a man without it being held in the greatest contempt. The women are not exposed as much as the men, and their tattooing is very inconsiderable. Their dress consists of a piece of cloth round their waists, answering to a short petticoat, and a mantle, which being tied on the left shoulder, and crossing the bosom, rests on the right hip, and hangs negligently as low as the knee, or calf of the leg, as it may accord with the taste of the lady. Their hair is generally black, but worn in different ways, some long, and turned up—others short. They are all fond of adorning their persons with flowers, and many of the wreaths are formed with such elegant simplicity, that does not contribute a little to their personal appearance, which is at all times particularly interesting; the beauty of their features being only equalled by the symmetry of their figures. They are of a bright copper colour, and in the cheeks of those who were requested to refrain from anointing themselves with oil, and the roots of trees, the crimson die was very conspicuous. In their early visits to the ship, they swam off, and as their clothes are not calculated to stand the water, they left them on the beach; but they never neglected taking with them a few leaves to tie round their waists. In this state of nature would they daily exhibit themselves, and too without suspecting, or being in the least degree conscious they were offering the most trivial offence to modesty. "Our first visitors," say the Missionary Voyages, "came off early from the shore; they were seven beautiful young women, swimming quite naked, except a few leaves round their middle; they kept playing round the ship for three hours, calling Wahēine, until several of the men came on board; one of whom being the Chief of the Island, requested that his sister might be taken on board, which was complied with: she was of a fair complexion, inclining to a healthy yellow, with a tint of red on her cheek, was rather stout, but possessing such symmetry of features, as did all her companions, that as models of Statuary and Painture their equal can seldom be found. Our Otaheitean girl who was tolerably fair, and had a comely person, was, notwithstanding, greatly eclipsed by these women, and I believe felt her inferiority in no small degree however, she was superior in the amiableness of her manners and possessed more of the softness and tender feeling of the sex: she was ashamed to see a woman upon the deck quite naked, and supplied her with a complete dress of new Otaheitean cloth, which set her off to great advantage, and encouraged those in the water, whose numbers were greatly increased, to importune for admission; and out of pity to them, as we saw they would not return, we took them on board, but they were in a measure disappointed, for they could not succeed so well as the first in getting clothed; nor did the mischievous goats even suffer them to keep their green leaves, but as they turned to avoid them they were attacked on each side alternately, and completely stripped naked."

I must confess, when I read this paragraph, notwithstanding the respectibility of the authority, I was rather inclined to be incredulous, but 'ere we had been at anchor many hours, a similar circumstance took place, and afterwards several others, and to which I was an eye witness.

Tattooing, or Patëkeë, is considered a great mark of distinction, the pain being of infinite accuteness, it shews what they are capable of

H

undergoing. There are many on whom it has been performed so often, that not a spot of their natural colour is seen to remain. Some are most fantastically done, although with great taste, and if it be possible, straight lines are always avoided. Those who are marked only sufficient to shew the class they belong to, are of the inferior order, or *toutous*, and have, perhaps, a fish, a bird, or something of little consequence, represented on one side of the face. The women, as I have before observed, are so little marked in this way that it seldom exceeds a hand, or a few fingers. The lips of many are streaked, and this is principally seen with those who are married, or have children, but it is not as many suppose a general rule among the married. The men are tall, well formed, muscular, and manly; possessing a great portion of vivacity and penetration; insomuch that for a people of whose language I was ignorant, I had less pains in making them understand me than any I ever met with. They took notice of every thing they saw, and I believe no one came on board who did not measure the length of the ship, and count the nnmber of guns, masts, decks, &c.

Their amusements are principally in dancing, swimming, and wrestling; throwing their javelins, and slinging stones, in the whole of which they are great proficients. Their arms consist of clubs, of which there are two kinds, the carved, and the plain, both made from a wood, though not hard when first cut, becomes so by being buried in the mud which serves as a strong die. Spears of 10 feet long, made from the same wood, or from the cocoa-nut tree, and slings made from grass. Bows and arrows have not yet been introduced among them. The stone from the sling is thrown a great distance, and with considerable accuracy.

The person of the king being tabooed, whatever place or ground he touches becomes sacred and to obviate the inconveniency to which his people would otherwise be subjected, he is at all times carried on a man's back, his conch, or horn, slung about his neck, and a small diadem, made of leaves, on his head. Several of the pricipal chiefs are in constant attendance, as well as a retinue of domestics. In his palace he has a canopy of state, under which he sits, or lies—there is great simplicity in its appearance. The palace is an open hut, situated near the sea-side, and has nothing, except its size, to distinguish it from any of the others. One of the rooms was curiously decorated with the skeleton heads of pigs, exceedingly clean, and well preserved. These animals, to a great number, had been sacrificed at the death of the king's mother, and whose heads were fixed round this apartment, by way of keeping her alive in his memory; but however dear she might have been to him, he did not hesitate to barter a couple of the best for an old razor.

Their candles are made by sticking a great number of the kernels of nuts on a long slip of bamboo, and from their oily nature, they are easily lit, burn very regular, and produce an exceedingly good light. There is a very small portion of smoke, and when the light is extinguished, the smell though rather powerful, is by no means disagreeable.

The quadrupeds consist only in pigs, and rats, the latter are exceedingly large, and in very great numbers, the pigs run wild, and are of a fine sort. I brought one of them to England with me, which being with young at the time of landing, I have now in my possession the species entire. The natives on seeing our cow, were much surprised, and called it a horned pig, not having seen any of the species before, or having the least idea what else it could be.

The natives of this place do not bleed their pigs, but strangle them with a rope, and after having taken out the entrails, and binding the body up with large leaves, it is laid on a heap of hot stones, which burns off the hair, and dresses the body; and had the one so prepared purposely for us by the Typees, in Comptrollers bay, been a little more dressed, I am persuaded no dish could have exceeded it: it was full of the richest gravy and was in every way calculated foi the exquisite palate of an alderman, who I am inclined to believe, would have taken it in preference, even to the callipee, or callepash, of the most delicious tortoise.

The cava, or spirits, drank here, possess very inebriating qualities, and bring on almost an immediate dizziness. It is produced from the leaves, and roots of a plant, which being chewed by women of the lower order, and spit into calabashes, or receivers, and mixed with the milk, from the cocoa-nut, is left to ferment; after which it is strained off, when it soon becomes fit for use. The kings, and a few chiefs, can alone afford to indulge themselves in this delicious nectar, and to those it produces a kind of dry scrofula in the skin, with soreness in the eyes, which was very conspicuous in the old king, for, notwithstanding he had undergone the ordeal of Tattooing to an immense degree, his skin was covered with such a dry white scale, that gave him, instead of a black, the appearance of being a light grey colour.

These people are seldom visited by sickness, which may in some measure be attributed to the simplicity of their diet, and their great attention to cleanliness. It is considered necessary with them to bathe at least three times a day, which greatly diminishes that sour offensive exhalation, proceding from those people of a similar climate, who are less attentive to their persons. In case of accidents, there are people who profess the art of surgery, and in setting fractures they are expert, aud successful. I saw but one operation of this nature, which was on a broken thigh—the swelling being reduced, the part fractured was bound carefully round with large leaves, when several splints, or smooth pieces of bamboo, were applied, which being bound with great caution, and the limb confined in one position, the operation was finished. One of the faculty was solicitous to be supplied with lancets, but I could not ascertain from Wilson, if phlebotomy had ever been practised, or if the old man understood the use of these instruments. However, he was furnished with enough to open all the veins in the Island.

Sir Thomas Staines taking great interest in

the voyage, and wishing to know beyond a vague conjecture, their mode of fighting, solicited the old king to cause a sham fight to be performed upon the plain, which he acceded to, and the old warrior, took great pleasure in going through all the various evolutions. For the club, a tolerably sized stick, was substituted—for the spear, a piece of bamboo, and the slingers, instead of stone, threw the small bread-fruit. Thus armed, about 300 of the most experienced went forth to the plain. The king, for the first time, was carried on a superb litter, which we had made for him on board. He gave direction to the chiefs, for the formation of both armies, which were drawn up in the following manner. About thirty principal warriors, with clubs, formed the first line—the second was composed of spearmen, and the slingers on the flanks. The battle commenced by a single combat between two chiefs, who displayed great powers, both in agility, and skill, and were struggling manfully when the signal was given to advance. A terrific and hideous shout followed. The slingers now began, but were obliged to retire on coming within the reach of the spears. The advance was rapid, and as the parties closed, so did the confusion increase. Club came in contact with club, and spear with spear,—the slingers stood aloof. The conch was at length sounded, when each party separated, the slingers, on either side, filing into the rear of their respective flanks to secure their retreat. They did not cease throwing stones until they were rendered of no effect. Both parties again drew up in their original order, and rested on their arms. The distance, as well as accuracy with which they throw a stone is almost incredible—the spearmen are also very expert. The countenances of many by being hit by shot from the slings, became quite ferocious—many were knocked down, but none received injury, and thus ended the representation of a battle, which must have been productive of great pleasure to every beholder.

The principal trees are bread-fruit and cocoanut, as from their produce the natives derive their subsistence, but there are various others, which together with a variety of plants and flowers, would afford the botanist an extensive field for speculation, and I regret to say I had no knowledge in so pleasing, as well as useful a science, or I certainly should have turned it to advantage. There are several fine streams of water, and ships may at all seasons be supplied without difficulty. There are also several mineral springs, but the qualities they possess I was wholly inadequate to ascertain.

The language spoken here, is by no means harsh, and principally formed from vowels, but I could not learn from Wilson, who is most egregiously ignorant, if like most others, it had any particular form, or government, or what it was, nor could I make myself sufficiently understood among the natives to ascertain it from them, but what I could collect, I shall here introduce, and I trust it will be not unacceptable. Their manner of counting is rather irregular, as they only count to twenty, and then the number of twenties, as will be seen by the following tables, to which I shall add, all the words, and expressions, we could gather during our stay, and which we found of great use.

A table of numerals used at the Island of Novaheevah Marquesas.

Atăchkee, *One*	Ahōno, *Six*
Ahōwā, *Two*	Ahēeto, *Seven*
Atoo, *Three*	Avāho, *Eight*
Ahā, *Four*	Ahēvā, *Nine*
Ahēmā, *Five*	Unāhoo, *Ten*

It will be necessary to observe, that the Eleventh number is formed by the addition of

I

"Om" to the first and the Twelfth by the same addition to the second, and so on to Twenty when they stop:—as

Omātachkee, *Eleven*	Omahonō, *Sixteen*
Omahōwa, *Twelve*	Omaheeto, *Seventeen*
Omatoo, *Thirteen*	Omavahō, *Eighteen*
Omāha, *Fourteen*	Omaheeva, *Nineteen*
Omahema, *Fifteen*	Omnahoo, *Twenty*

To count a greater number than Twenty, they would say for the first "Atachkee Omnahoo" and commence afresh with the first number, and "Ahōwa Omnahoo" would be the second twenty, or forty, and so on: but they are by no means expert in any kind of calculation.

The following phrases we found of considerable use.

English.	*Marquesean.*
How do you do?	*Cāovākooe.*
Very well.	*Nue nue moee tackey.*
Give me something to eat.	*Toko mi te kiee.*
to drink.	*Toko mi te māāha ĕnee.*
I will give you.	*Tou he toko atoo.*
Come here.	*Pee mi.*
I am coming.	*Anā aoe.*
I do not understand.	*Coree aoyocō.*

What do you say?	*Ayahā.*
What do you want?	*Eno waku?*
Do you like me?	*Atee me tackey wowney.*
Yes.	*Ihee.*
Then give me a kiss?	*Pee me tee toee.*
By and bye.	*Apo.*
Do not make a noise.	*Too weetoo wee.*
It is not me.	*Coree aoee.*
You lie.	*Te vā vā.*
Will you go on board?	*A moce tu owā tiee?*
No.	*Coree.*
Give me a spear.	*Toko me packahoo.*
The day after to-morrow.	*Oheyohee-ēhiee.*
My love.	*Vihence now.*
Go away.	*Fetee.*
Kiss me.	*Ho kee my day sho.*
Be off.	*Ta ha too.*
Go to sleep.	*A moce.*
You kill, or hurt me.	*Me mate! me mate!*
I will knock your brains out.	*Tororo. (an expression of great anger)*
Give me some bread.	*Py my ti ti potata.*
Give me some water.	*Py my viee.*
I am dying of hunger.	*Me mate de owney.*
The barbarous Porter killed the Typees.	*Teekeeno Porter mate mate Typee. (a general expression.*

A list of words we collected during our stay at Port Anna Maria.

A

Axe, *Tokee*
Arms, *Ema*

B

Britain, (Great) *Pic-tatane.*
Bad, *Tekeeno*
Bird, *Manoo*
Boat, *Waca*
Ball, *Keeva*
Belly, *Apowe*
Bread, *Potato*

C

Club, *Acaootoowāh*
Cocoa-nut, *Iahee*
Cloth, *Cahoo*
Cloth girdle, *Āmee*
Carved club, *Hoohoo*

D

Dog, *Patoo*
Devil, *Vihenee ihee*

E

Eyes, *Kecco mata*
England, *Picatance*

F

Face, *Mata*
Fish, *Eca*
Fish, (large) *Eca nue*
Fire, *ha-hee*
File, *Cookhee*
Foul, *mowa*
Fish-hook, *Pekee*

G

God *Eātooā*
Ghost, *Atoowa*
Good, *Mocc tackee*

H

Hunger, *Owney*
Hut, *Afiee*
Hair, *Wohoo*

K

Kill, *Mate*

L

Legs, *Etee mie*
Large, *Nue nue*
Light, *Hama*
Louse, *Hootoo*

M

Many, *Attee*

Man, *Vahānā*
More, *To tackey*
Musket, *Poohee*

N

No, *Coree*
Nothing, *Ahohwee*

P

Powder, *Hoeecock*
Paint, (red) *Anamor*
Pig, *Powaca*

R

Red cloth, *Cahoo a-namor*
Rat, *Keckoo*
Rain, *Owa*

S

Small, *Etee*
Something, *Mayahah*
Ship, *Waca nue*
Spirits, *Viee kavā*
Swim, *Cowte tiee*
Stone, *Cayā*
Spear, *Pakaao*
Sling, *Maca*

T

Teeth, *Na yeu*
To-morrow, *Ohhe-eohee*
Tattooing, *Patikee*
Toutou, *Servant*
Tayo, *Brother*

Water, *Viee*
Wind, *Matanee*
Woman, *Waheene*

Y

Yes, *Ihee*

The marvellous stories related by the American Officers, who had been taken in the Essex, and who were at Valparàiso, when we arrived there, relative to the ferociousness of the people, inhabiting the interior of this Island, had greatly excited my curiosity, and 'ere we reached Port Anna Maria, I had made up my mind to ascertain beyond a doubt, whether the terrific description given of them was correct; and to accomplish this point, a party of several officers was made, and every arrangement necessary for crossing the mountains entered into: however, when the period came, from causes which I cannot explain, we were reduced from the number of a dozen to only three; namely Lieut. J. Morgan, commanding the Marines of the Tagus, Mr. Blackmore, Midshipman of the Briton, and myself. To these gentlemen I shall ever feel myself obliged; for had they forsaken me also, I should not have relinquished the journey, but have gone alone, and their company and observations were throughout the day, both agreeable, and interesting. It was soon after day-light when we set out, accompanied by my Tayo Patookee, as a guide, and Otaheitan Jack as interpreter.

In the two preceding days to our journey, a considerable quantity of rain had fallen, and the road which bore the appearance of being always bad, was now become almost impassible, insomuch, that each step we ascended, the difficulty increased, and in many places, and for several yards together, the mountain was so steep, that had it not been for the roots of trees, forming themselves into steps, any attempt to cross by this route would have been vain.—About nine o'clock we reached the summit, where we tarried awhile, not only to take some refreshment, but to gaze on the various beauties of nature as they presented themselves. It was impossible to turn the eye, where it was not met by the most romantic scenery.

We had now full three miles farther to walk, before we could reach the country of the reputed Cannibals, and as the road did not bear a very favorable appearance, we hastened our departure from the spot, and proceeded on our journey—we had not gone far before we were met by some natives, inhabiting the small, though comparatively level district, through which we were passing, who brought us cocoa nuts, and demonstrated their joy, and friendship, by a number of strange actions, which pleased the more because it augured a favorable reception from the Typees. This country is of a deep rich soil, and capable of the greatest improvement. The cocoa-nut, and bread-fruit trees, are every where conspicuous.—There are also some sandle trees found here.

It was nearly noon before we completed our journey, (about 10 miles from the port) when we were received, and treated with great kindness by those terrific people, whom Captain Porter speaks of as having conquered and rendered tributary to the American flag. The whole seemed pleased, and their satisfaction at seeing us was expressed in various ways, some danced, others sang, knelt down, embraced us, with many other laughable actions, which would be impossible for me to describe. They anticipated our wishes in every thing. The cocoa-nut for our refreshment was presented us, as well as clubs, spears, slings, &c. &c. as pledges of their regard, and which they caused one of their people to carry even to the ship. They examined every thing we had with us, and were greatly astonished at the whiteness of our skin; several of them opened the bosom of my shirt, the sleeves of my coat, the bottoms of my trowsers, and one was even so incredulous as to wash my hand to ascertain if it was not painted. At this time, we were in the place of assembly, surrounded by more than five hundred of them, and I must confess I did not like so strict an examination, which was however put a stop to by my friend Morgan, who with Mr. Blackmore, was undergoing a similar process. At his discharging a pistol in the air, the whole assembly fell prostrate, and in which attitude they remained a considerable time, or until they thought the shot had reached its destination. When they were about to rise, a second was fired, which was productive of the same effect. This scene was so truly ludicrous, that to have withheld from laughing would have been morally impossible. When they had recovered, at their request, the pistols were several times discharged but during the rest of the day; every one observed the most accommodating distance. I have not the most trivial thought of their having been actuated by aught but curiosity, for had they entertained a hostile thought, our being armed with pistols would not have intimidated them; we were so few in number, that one volley of stones, from their slingers, would have given them quiet possession of our bodies. On this occasion I received great assistance from my Tayo Patookee, as well as on every other, during the whole period of our stay in the Island.

The Morais of this place, like those of Tuliony, are by no means handsome, but the square of public assembly is much superior, and sufficiently spacious to contain 1200 people: it is also well built. The manners and customs of this tribe, appear in every respect the same as those at the Port, or Tuhuony. The land is very luxuriant, but nothing is propagated; save the few trees from whose fruits they subsist, and which almost grow spontaneous. There is not any sugar cane, though it would flourish throughout the Island. In the mountains I saw several small birds of a beauteous plumage, but they are not plenty.

It was here these poor, but friendly people, complained in the most bitter terms of the barbarity they had experienced from Captain Porter, and pointed out the spot where he came with a devastating and ruthless hand, and not content with burning their villages, and destroying their trees, shot cold bloodedly, fourteen of their defenceless brethren. In speaking of him their countenances became quite ferocious, and "Te keeno Porter maté, maté, Typee," or the "*wicked and brutal Porter murdered the Typees,*" resounded throughout the circle. Their joy at hearing he was taken a prisoner, was excessive, and expressed by the most hideous grimaces. One of them, to explain more fully to the rest that he was a prisoner, tied his legs with his sling, and the pleasure this diffused, was not only conspicuous in every face, but proved that this gentleman's conduct had by no means kept pace with the dignity of a civilized nation, nor reflected honour on America; and that in the account given of him at Port Anna Maria, there had been no exaggeration.

I strove with assiduity to ascertain if he

really had not some cause which might be adduced in extenuation, but no clue could I find to any thing, having a tendency to qualify his conduct. Cocoa-nuts they brought him in great abundance, as well as the greater part of their pigs. He demanded more, to which they found it impossible to accede, without great injury being done to their breeding stock: but this they were obliged to do to prevent the farther effusion of blood. This point accomplished, Captain Porter returns in triumph to the port, laden with his trophies and booty, where he is hailed the great, the magnanimous conqueror!!*

The reader will, I am satisfied, feel great indignation at conduct so repugnant to human nature, and in opposition to civilization; but more particularly so when he finds that the

* After the return of Captain Porter from this horrible slaughter, which had terminated in a manner so disgraceful to the arms of America, he caused a throne to be erected in his cabin, on which he sat to receive the homage of those people whom he had rendered tributary to the American flag. On which occasion he styled himself king. This I had from Wilson, our interpreter, who was himself present at this bombastical coronation, which would be ridiculous under any circumstances, but more particularly so in a subject of a Republican Government.

people against whom this ruthless sham king* carried war, with all its horrors, are in his own declaration to the world, declared to be defenceless.

The day was far advanced, and neither of us being desirous to spend the night in so remote a place, we turned our thoughts upon re-crossing the mountains, which we found infinitely more tedious than in the ascent. A great concourse accompanied us to the summit, when we parted, and I must confess, I returned on on board not less delighted with my journey, than satisfied that the tales I had before heard relative to the Typees, had not the smallest claim to veracity.

I shall now give a brief sketch of what passed at Tuhuony during the period of the Essex's stay there, as well as the ultimate fate of the prizes she took with her, but before I proceed farther, I will lay before the reader a couple of paragraphs from a written document which Captain Porter caused to be buried under the

---

* This is the man who caused a British subject (who was on board his ship, and would not enter and serve against his country in war) to be stripped naked, tarred, feathered, and sent on shore in Boston!!! He is also the person who has been eulogized by Mr. Cobbet!

flag staff, and which was dug for and found in a bottle by our men. It contained also one silver and two copper coins of the United States. The paper ran thus:—

CAPTAIN PORTER's DECLARATION.

"It is hereby made known to the world, that I David Porter, a Captain in the Navy of the United States of America, and now in command of the United States Frigate Essex, have on the part of the said United States, taken possession of the Island called by the natives Nooahcevah, generally known by the name of Sir Henry Martyn's Island, but now called Maddison's Island; that by the request and assistance of the Friendly tribes residing in the valley of Tuhuony, as well as the tribes residing in the Mountains, whom I have conquered and rendered tributary to our flag, I have caused the village of Maddison to be built, consisting of six convenient houses, a rope walk, bakery, and other appurtenances; and for the protection of the same, I have constructed a fort calculated to mount sixteen guns, whereon I have mounted four, and have called the same Fort Maddison.

"Presents, consisting of the produce of the Island to a great amount have been brought in by every tribe in the Island, not excepting the most remote." Here he goes on to enumerate the tribes, after which he says, "Our right to this Island being founded on priority of discovery, conquest, and possession, cannot be disputed; but the natives to secure themselves that friendly protection which their defenceless situation so much required, have requested to be admitted into the great American Family; whose pure republican policy approaches so near their own, and, in order to encourage those views to their own interest and happiness, as well as to render secure our claim to an Island, valuable on so many considerations, I have taken upon myself to promise them they shall be so adopted; that our chief shall be their chief, and they having given me assurances that such of their brethren, as may hereafter visit them from the United States, shall enjoy a welcome and hospitable reception among them, and be furnished with whatever refreshments and supplies the Island may afford; that they will protect them against their enemies, and as far as lays in their power will prevent the subjects of Great Britain (knowing them to be such) from coming among them until peace shall take place between the two nations."

The remainder of this document is quite uninteresting, but it was signed by Captain

Porter, and the whole of the officers belonging to the Essex.

From this document it appears, that this royal personage on his arrival, thought it expedient to take possession of an eminence, and on it to erect a battery for the protection of the people, who were at work in the plain below. Town Maddison too, was constructed, as well as a wall, not mentioned in any part of his declaration, inclosing his camp, which now stands as a lasting monument of his barbarity. The fort was demolished, and Town Maddison burnt immediately after his departure from the Island, and this wall, notwithstanding his silence on the subject in his declaration to the world, having some claim to attention, must not be left unnoticed. It is about 5 feet high, built of stone, and incloses an oblong of nearly 600 yards of ground, and was constructed by the English prisoners, who were obliged to work, either at building, or carrying stone, during the whole period of its completion, in the heat of the day, and disgracefully loaded with irons. But to explain this more fully, it will be necessary for me to use the words of Mr. Watson, a Captain of one of the Whalers, who, when he was shewing me these instruments of tyranny, expressed himself in the following manner:—"Yes, Sir, in these irons I have carried many a load of stone, and if you ever go to Port Anna Maria, you will probably see a wall which I participated in building. We had men to attend us with whips, nor were we allowed to carry this shot under our arm, but made to drag it after us. I will never part with them while I live, and when I get home, I will have them fixed in a case, for the gratification of those who may wish to see them." This is as near the relation as I could recollect, when I returned on board to give it a place in my journal. He related several other cruel hardships which he had been subjected to, but as I think a sufficient sample has been given of this self-created Monarch's humanity, I proceed with my narrative.

It here, perhaps, may not be improper to pay that tribute to the character of Captain Lownes (the then first Lieut. of the Essex) which he seems so justly entitled to.—Throughout the whole, he appears to have been a generous fellow, and as much as laid in his power to have alleviated the distresses of the prisoners. They spoke of him in very high terms.

The Essex sailed from Nooaheevah, leaving their prizes in charge of Lieut. Gamble, of the marines, who has been pointed out to me as a more cruel, and merciless tyrant than even His

Drawn & Etch'd by J. Shillibeer

The Master of an English Whaler shewing the Irons in which Captⁿ Porter caused him to work when at the Island of Nooaheevah.

Majesty the Captain himself. This Gentleman remained in the port some time subsequent to the departure of the Essex, but his conduct being the occasion of several desertions, and thereby being weakened, he hastened his departure. He was preparing the Greenwich for his reception, and had moved the prisoners on board the ship he lived in: these embraced the earliest opportunity of rising, and Mr. Gamble was seized, put into irons, and afterwards flogged with six dozen on the back, in retaliation for the nnmber of lashes he had wantonly bestowed on them. The English, with a few Americans who had joined them, put immediately to sea, taking Mr. Gamble with them, and when nearly out of sight of land, they put him into a boat with only a broken oar, and bid him get back if he could—he was also shot at, and wounded in the heel:—however, he succeeded in regaining the Island, when he found his situation very alarming, his crew by desertion being greatly reduced, and not a native in his favor. He therefore sent an armed boat to the shore; to bring off what little was there remaining, and also to plunder the harbour and Wilson, who had refused to take a part against the natives; but fortune still in opposition to his views, whilst they were employed at this amiable work, the

L

boat was thrown on the beach by the surf, and the men, anxious to get her again afloat, unthinkingly left their arms, when a party of natives who were in ambush, rushed in upon them, and in an instant Mr. Feltus, a midshipman, and two men, were laid dead on the beach: the rest succeeded in swimming off to the ship, but not without carrying with them some severe bruises which they had received from the stones. Mr. Gamble's case now became extremely serious, and dreading an attack from the shore, he set fire to the Greenwich, cut his own cables, and put to sea, and bending his course towards Owhyhee, he arrived there just in time to be taken possession of by His Majesty's sloop Cherub, who brought him in safety to Valparaiso. Thermometer on board 84°, on shore 100° to 105°.

By the consent of all the tribes assembled, excepting the Typees, (who declared they would make no concession, or acknowledgement, to any power) the Island was taken possession of in the name of his Britannic Majesty. A royal salute was fired from the Briton and Tagus, and the Union displayed on a flagstaff at the Palace Royal. This was a parting ceremony, and early next morning we weighed anchor, and proceeded to the Island of Christiana, where we arrived on the 31st,

(next day) and anchored in a small bay to the eastward of Resolution bay. Here we were soon visited by some of the natives, whose manners and customs we found similar to those of Novaheevah, excepting a great propensity to thieving, and a trifling difference in some of their words. The scenery of this place like that of the other Islands has an exceedingly wild and romantic appearance.—The mountains high, steep, and covered with foliage of most luxuriant nature. The land is very rich, and, like Novaheevah, capable of every improvement.

At this Island, Crook, one of the missionary Gentlemen, was left by Captain Wilson, but I believe he did not remain long enough to work any particular good among the natives. His house was in a retired spot, near the bank of a river, about a mile from the shore. It bore no trace of ever having been the residence of a European. He was much esteemed.

The water here is good, and ships may be supplied with ease, though not with great expedition. It was here one of Mr. Gamble's men, (Peter Snack,) joined us, who complained greatly of that gentleman's conduct, which he declared was the sole and onl cause of his desertion. I do not imagine he entered on board the Briton with a view of serving against his country, but merely to ensure a passage back, his conduct during his stay on board was exemplary. This man corroborated the story of Captain Porter's coronation.

The natives of this Island were labouring under the influence of an intermittent fever and ague, for which was administered both as a remedy and antidote, the juice of the leaves of certain trees and berries, and which was attended with great success. Boyce, a boy 14 years old, deserted here.

Our curiosity being now pretty well satiated, for we had seen every thing worthy of notice, on the morning of the 2d September we took our final departure from these friendly people, and as this chapter has been rather long, I shall leave the reader to rest awhile, and the interesting incident which transpired on our voyage back to the Continent, he will find related in the ensuing one.

CHAPTER V.

Having sailed from the Marquesas, it will be necessary for me to take a cursory view of Mr. Bligh's voyage to Otaheite, in 1788, about which period he was appointed to the command of the Bounty, with a Mr. Christian as his Chief Mate, or First Lieutenant, for the purpose of conveying the bread-fruit tree to the West Indies. The progress he made in his undertaking—his sailing from Otaheite—the subsequent mutiny—the entire annihilation of the object of his voyage, and the miraculous return to the coast of Timor, in an open boat, are circumstances so well known, and have been so feelingly described, that at the very name of the BOUNTY, they must recur with such strength to any reflective mind, that it will be needless for me to touch on the conduct of the unfortunate young man, who led that much to be lamented conspiracy, or that of the experienced Navigator, who appears to have been the chief object of their hatred, and I am afraid the sole cause of the unjustifiable conduct used towards him.

For many years, the ultimate fate of Christian was uncertain, and the prevailing opinion was, that after he had left and destroyed the Bounty, he returned to the coast of S. America, and entered into the Spanish service; nay, it has even been asserted, he had been recognized in that situation, and after the account given of him by Mayhew Folgier,* there were many who retained the same opinion; but the matter is at present too clearly demonstrated to admit of a doubt, and those idle tales must now meet the fate they then merited.

The following account is given in the Missionary Voyage, of the conduct of the Mutineers at, and their departure from Otaheite, since which period to the time of Captain Folgier's touching at Pitcairnes, every thing relative to those infatuated men has been but a vague conjecture.

"The wind blew fresh from Toubouai and the intention of our Captain was not to go near this Island; but for the sake of some who were desirous of seeing it, we tacked to windward, and towards evening got within a few miles of it; he thought it not prudent to land on account of the natives being prejudiced against the English, through the Mutineers of the Bounty, who had destroyed near a hundred of them.

* The master of the first ship which touched at Pitcairnes Island.

" This Island was discovered by Captain Cook, in the year 1777, and upon it the unhappy Fletcher Christian, with his companions, the Mutineers of the Bounty, attempted a settlement in 1789. They had with them some natives of Otaheite, and live stock of different sorts. Notwithstanding the opposition they met with from the natives on their first arrival, they warped the ship through the only opening in the reef; then landed, chose a spot of ground, built a fort thereon, and taking their live stock on shore, they intended, had the natives proved friendly to their stay, to have destroyed the Bounty and fixed themselves there: but their own unruly conduct alienated the natives from them, who withheld their women, which they were ready to seize by violence: they excited the jealousy of the chiefs by a friendship formed with one in preference to the rest; they were disunited amongst themselves, and many longed for Otaheite: they resolved to leave Toubouai, for and carry with them all they live stock which had brought, the benefit of which the Toubouians began to understand, and were unwilling to see them again all collected and removed. This caused the first brawl between the Otaheitean servants, who were driving in the hogs, and the natives. Insolence, and want of gentleness, and conciliation, led to all the bloody consequences which ensued. The natives were numerous, and fought with great courage, forcing the Mutineers, to avail themselves of a high ground, where with their superior skill, and the advantage of fire-arms, and the aid of the Otaheiteans, who fought bravely on this occasion, they at last came off victorious, with only two of themselves wounded, whilst the dead bodies of the Toubouians covered the spot; and were afterwards thrown up in three or four heaps, Thus finding that no peaceable settlement was now to be obtained in this place, they shipped their live stock, abandoned their fort, and taking their friendly chief on board with them, weighed anchor and steered towards Matavai bay, in the Island of Otaheite. On their passage thither it is said Christian became very melancholy, confining himself to his cabin, and would hardly speak a word to any person; lamenting most probably, that the resolutions he had formed without deliberation, and executed with rash haste, had now involved his life, and those of his adherents in misery. As soon as they anchored in Matavai bay in Otaheite, those who wished to stay there went on shore; but nine of the Mutineers, and also some of the native men and women remained on

board. With these Christian cutting the cable in the night, put to sea, and steering to the N. W. has never been heard of since."

We left the friendly Marquesians on the 2d of September, and were proceeding on our voyage to regain the port of Valparaiso, steering a course which ought, according to the charts and every other authority, to have carried us nearly 3 degrees of longitude to the eastward of Pitcairn's Island, and our surprize was greatly excited by its sudden and unexpected appearance. It was in the second watch when we made it. At day light we proceeded to a more close examination, and soon perceived huts, cultivation, and people; of the latter, some were making signs, others launching their little canoes through the surf, into which they threw themselves with great dexterity, and pulled towards us.

At this moment I believe neither Captain Bligh of the Bounty, nor Christian, had entered any of our thoughts, and in waiting the approach of the strangers, we prepared to ask them some questions in the language of those people we had so recently left. They came—and for me to picture the wonder which was conspicuous in every countenance, at being hailed in perfect English, what was the name of the ship, and who commanded her, would

M

be impossible—our surprize can alone be conceived. The Captain answered, and now a regular conversation commenced. He requested them to come alongside, and the reply was, "We have no boat hook to hold on by." "I will throw you a rope" said the Captain. "If you do we have nothing to make it fast to" was the answer. However, they at length came on board, exemplifying not the least fear, but their astonishment was unbounded.

After the friendly salutation of good morrow, Sir, from the first man who entered (Mackey) for that was his name, "Do you know, said he, one William Bligh, in England? This question threw a new light on the subject, and he was immediately asked if he knew one Christian, and the reply was given with so much natural simplicity, that I shall here use his proper words. "Oh yes," said he, "very well, his son is in the boat there coming up, his name is Friday Fletcher October Christian. His father is dead now—he was shot by a black fellow." Several of them had now reached the ship, and the scene was become exceedingly interesting, every one betrayed the greatest anxiety to know the ultimate fate of that misled young man, of whose end so many vague reports had been in circulation, and those who did not ask questions, devoured with avidity every word which led to an elucidation of the mysterious termination of the unfortunate Bounty.

The questions which were now put were numerous, and as I am inclined to believe their being arranged with their specific answers, will convey to the reader, the circumstance as it really took place, with greater force than a continued relation, I shall adopt that plan, and those occurrences which did not lead immediately to the end of Christian, and the establishment of the colony, I will relate faithfully as they transpired.

Question.—Christian you say was shot?

Answer.—Yes he was.

Q.—By whom?

A.—A black fellow shot him.

Q,—What cause do you assign for the murder.

A.—I know no reason, except a jealousy which I have heard then existed between the people of Otaheite and the English—Christian was shot in the back while at work in his yam plantation.

Q.—What became of the man who killed him?

A.—Oh! that black fellow was shot afterwards by an Englishman.

Q.—Was there any other disturbance between the Otahetians and English, after the death of Christian?

A.—Yes, the black fellows rose, shot two Englishmen, and wounded John Adams, who is now the only remaning man who came in the Bounty.

Q.—How did Adams escape being murdered?

A.—He hid himself in the wood, and the same night, the women enraged at the murder of the English, to whom they were more partial than their countrymen, rose and put every Otahetian to death in their sleep. This saved Adams, his wounds were soon healed, and although old, he now enjoys good health.

Q.—How many men and women did Christian bring with him in the Bounty?

A.—Nine white men, six from Otaheite, and eleven women.

Q.—And how many are there now on the Island?

A.—In all we have 48.

Q.—Have you ever heard Adams say how long it is since he came to the Island?

A.—I have heard it is about 25 years ago.

Q.—And what became of the Bounty?

A.—After every thing useful was taken out of her, she was run on shore, set fire to, and burnt.

Q.—Have you ever heard how many years it is since Christian was shot?

A.—I understand it was about two years after his arrival at the Island.

Q.—What became of Christian's wife?

A.—She died soon after Christian's son was born, and I have heard that Christian took forcibly the wife of one of the black fellows to supply her place, and which was the chief cause of his being shot.

Q.—Then, Fletcher October Christian is the oldest on the Island, except John Adams, and the old women?

A.—Yes he is the first born on the Island.

Q.—At what age do you marry?

A.—Not before 19 or 20.

Q.—Are you allowed to have more than one wife?

A.—No! we can have but one, and it is wicked to have more.

Q.—Have you been taught any religion?

A.—Yes, a very good religion.

Q.—In what do you believe?

A.—I believe in God the Father Almighty, &c. (Here he went through the whole of the Belief.)

Q.—Who first taught you this Belief?

A.—John Adams says it was first by F.

Christian's order, and that he likewise caused a prayer to be said every day at noon.

Q.—And what is the prayer?

A.—It is,—"I will arise and go to my father, and say unto him Father, I have sinned against Heaven, and before thee, and am no more worthy of being called thy son."

Q.—Do you continue to say this every day?

A.—Yes, we never neglect it.

Q.—What language do you commonly speak?

A.—Always English.

Q.—But you understand the Otahetian?

A.—Yes, but not so well.

Q.—Do the old women speak English?

A.—Yes, but not so well as they understand it, their pronunciation is not good.

Q.—What countrymen do you call yourselves?

A.—Half English, and half Otaheite.

Q.—Who is your King?

A.—Why, King George to be sure.

Q.—Have you ever seen a ship before?

A.—Yes, we have seen four from the Island, but only one stopped. Mayhew Folgier was the Captain, I suppose you know him?—No, we do not know him.

Q.—How long did he stay?

A.—Two days.

Q.—Should you like to go to England?

A.—No! I cannot, I am married, and have a family.

Before we had finished our interrogatories the hour of breakfast had arrived, and we solicited our half countrymen, as they styled themselves, to accompany us below, and partake of our repast, to which they acquiesced without much ceremony. The circle in which we had surrounded them being opened, brought to the notice of Mackey, a little black terrier. He was at first frightened, ran behind one of the officers, and looking over his shoulder said, pointing to the dog, "I know what that is, it is a dog, I never saw a dog before—will it bite?" After a short pause he addressed himsef to Christian, saying with great admiration, "It is a pretty thing too to look at, is it not?"

The whole of them were inquisitive, and in their questions as well as answers, betrayed a very great share of natural abilities.

They asked the names of whatever they saw, and the purposes to which it was applied. This, they would say, was pretty,—that they did not like, and were greatly surprised at our having so many things which they were not possessed of in the Island.

The circumstance of the dog, the things

which at each step drew their attention or created their wonder, retarded us on our road to the breakfast table, but arriving there, we had a new cause for surprize. The astonishment which before had been so strongly demonstrated in them, was now become conspicuous in us, even to a much greater degree than when they hailed us in our native language ; and I must here confess I blushed when I saw nature in its most simple state, offer that tribute of respect to the Omnipotent Creator, which from an education I did not perform, nor from society had been taught its necessity. 'Ere they began to eat ; on their knees, and with hands uplifted did they implore permission to partake in peace what was set before them, and when they had eaten heartily, resuming their former attitude, offered a fervent prayer of thanksgiving for the indulgence they had just experienced. Our omission of this ceremony did not escape their notice, for Christian asked me whether it was not customary with us also. Here nature was triumphant, for I should do myself an irreparable injustice, did I not with candour acknowledge, I was both embarrassed and wholly at a loss for a sound reply, and evaded this poor fellow's question by drawing his attention to the cow, which was then looking down the hatchway, and as he had never seen any of the species before, it was a source of mirth and gratification to him.

The hatred of these people to the blacks is strongly rooted, and which doubtless owes its origin to the early quarrels which Christian and his followers had with the Otahetians after their arrival at Pitcarnes ; to illustrate which I shall here relate an occurrence which took place at breakfast.

Soon after young Christian had began, a West Indian Black, who was one of the servants, entered the gun-room to attend table as usual. Christian looked at him sternly, rose, asked for his hat, and said, "I don't like that black fellow, I must go," and it required some little persuasion, 'ere he would again resume his seat. The innocent Quashe was often reminded of the anecdote by his fellow servants.

After coming along side the ship, so eager were they to get on board, that several of the canoes had been wholly abandoned, and gone adrift, This was the occasion of an anecdote which will show most conspicuously the good nature of their dispositions, and the mode resorted to in deciding a double claim. The canoes being brought back to the ship, the Captain ordered that one of them should remain in each, when it became a question to

N

which that duty should devolve; however it was soon adjusted, for Mackey observed that he supposed they were all equally anxious to see the ship, and the fairest way would be for them to cast lots, as then there would be no ill will on either side. This was acceded to, and those to whom it fell to go into the boat, departed without a murmur.

I could wish it had been possible for us to have prolonged our stay for a few days, not only for our own gratification, but for the benefit which these poor people would have derived from it, for I am perfectly satisfied, from the interest every one took, nothing would have been withheld by the lowest of the crew which probability told him would add to their comfort: however this was impossible; for, from some cause on the part of the commissariat department, and which I cannot well explain, we were reduced to so comparatively small a portion of provisions, that it was necessary to use every means to expedite our return to South America, and after ascertaining the longitude to be in 130° 25′, W. and latitude 25° 4′S. we again set sail and proceeded on our voyage.

No one but the Captains went ashore, which will be a source of lasting regret to me, for I would rather have seen the simplicity of that little village, than all the splendour and magnificence of a city.

I now lament it the more, because the conclusion of this chapter will be from the relation of another, and I was willing to lay as little as possible before the reader, but to what I had myself been a witness; still, as I can rely on its veracity, I shall hope it will please. "After landing" said my friend "and we had ascended a little eminence, we were imperceptibly led through groupes of cocoa-nuts and bread-fruit trees, to a beantiful picturesque little village, formed on an oblong square, with trees of various kinds irregularly interspersed. The houses small, but regular, convenient, and of unequalled cleanliness. The daughter of Adams, received us on the hill. She came doubtlessly as a spy, and had we taken men, or even been armed ourselves, would certainly have given her father timely notice to escape, but as we had neither, she waited our arrival, and conducted us to where her father was. She was arrayed in nature's simple garb, and wholly unadorned, but she was beauty's self, and needed not the aid of ornament. She betrayed some surprize—timidity was a prominent feature.

"John Adams is a fine looking old man, approaching to sixty years of age. We conversed with him a long time, relative to the mutiny of the Bounty, and the ultimate fate of Christian. He denied being accessary to, or having the least knowledge of the conspiracy, but he expressed great horror at the conduct of Captain Bligh, not only towards his men, but officers also. I asked him if he had a desire to return to England, and I must confess his replying in the affirmative, caused me great surprize.

"He told me he was perfectly aware how deeply he was involved; that by following the fortune of Christian, he had not only sacrificed every claim to his country, but that his life, was the necessary forfeiture for such an act, and he supposed would be exacted from him was he ever to return: notwithstanding all these circumstances, nothing would be able to occasion him so much gratification as that of seeing once more, prior to his death, that country which gave him birth, and from which he had been so long estranged.

"There was a sincerity in his speech, I can badly describe it—but it had a very powerful influence in persuading me these were his real sentiments. My interest was excited to so great a degree, that I offered him a conveyance for himself, with any of his family who chose to accompany him. He appeared pleased at the proposal, and as no one was then present, he sent for his wife and children. The rest of this little community surrounded the door. He communicated his desire, and solicited their aquiescence. Appalled at a request not less sudden than in opposition to their wishes, they were all at a loss for a reply.

His charming daughter although inundated with tears, first broke the silence.

"Oh do not, Sir," said she "take from me my father! do not take away my best—my dearest friend." Her voice failed her—she was unable to proceed—lent her head upon her hand, and gave full vent to her grief. His wife too (an Otaheitian) expressed a lively sorrow. The wishes of Adams soon became known among the others, who joined in pathetic solicitation for his stay on the Island. Not an eye was dry—the big tear stood in those of the men—the women shed them in full abundance. I never witnessed a scene so fully affecting, or more replete with interest. To have taken him from a circle of such friends, would have ill become a feeling heart, to have forced him away in opposition to their joint and earnest entreaties, would have been an outrage on humanity.

"With assurances that it was neither our wish nor intention to take him from them against his inclination, their fears were at length dissipated. His daughter too had gained her usual serenity, but she was lovely in her tears, for each seemed to add an additional charm. Forgetting the unhappy deed which placed Adams in that spot, and seeing him only in the character he now is, at the head of a little community, adored by all, instructing all, in religion, industry, and friendship, his situation might be truly envied, and one is almost inclined to hope that his unremitting attention to the government and morals of this extraordinary little colony, will ultimately, prove an equivalent for the part he formerly took,—entitle him to praise, and should he ever return to England, ensure him the clemency of that Sovereign he has so much injured"

The young women have invariably beautiful teeth, fine eyes, and open expression of countenances, and looks of such simple innocence, and sweet sensibility, that renders their appearance at once interesting and engaging, and it is pleasing to add, their minds and manners were as pure and innocent, as this impression indicated. No lascivious looks, or any loose, forward manners, which so much distinguish the characters of the females of the other Islands.

The Island itself has an exceedingly pretty

appearance, and I was informed by Christian, every part was fertile and capable of being cultivated. The coast is every way bound with rocks, insomuch that they are at all times obliged to carry their little boats to the village, but the timber is of so light a nature that one man is adequate to the burden of the largest they have.

Each family has a separate allotment of land, and each strive to rival the other in their agricultural pursuits, which is chiefly confined to the propagation of the Yam, and which they have certainly brought to the finest perfection I ever saw. The bread-fruit and cocoa-nut trees, were brought with them in the Bounty, and have been since reared with great success. The pigs also came by the same conveyance, as well as goats and poultry. They had no pigeons, and I am sorry to say no one thought of leaving those few we had on board, with them.

The pigs have got into the woods, and many are now wild. Fish of various sorts are taken here, and in great abundance ; the tackling is all of their own manufacturing, and the hooks, although beat out of old iron hoops, not only answer the purpose, but are fairly made.

Needles they also make from the same materials. Those men who came on board, were finely formed, and of manly features. Their height about 5 feet 10 inches. Their hair black and long, generally plaited into a tail.

They wore a straw hat, similar to those worn by sailors, with a few feathers stuck into them by way of ornament. On their shoulders was a mantle resembling the Chilinan Poncho which hung down to the knee, and round the waist, a girdle corresponding to that of the Indians at the Marquesas, both of which are produced from the bark of trees growing on the Islands. They told me they had clothes on shore, but never wore them. I spoke to Christian particularly, of Adams, who assured me he was greatly respected, insomuch that no one acted in opposition to his wishes, and when they should lose him, their regret would be general. The inter-marriages which had taken place among them, have been the occasion of a relationship throughout the colony. There seldom happens to be a quarrel, even of the most trivial nature, and then, (using their own term,) is nothing more than a word of mouth quarrel, which is always referred to Adams for adjustment.

Several books belonging to Captain Bligh which were taken out of the Bounty were then in the possession of Adams, and the first voyage of Captain Cook was brought on board

Friday Fletcher October Christian

Drawn & Etched by J Shillibeer

the Briton. In the title page of each volume the name of Captain Bligh was written, and I suppose in his own writing. Christian had written his name immediately under it without running his pen through, or defacing in the least that of Captain Bligh's. On the margins of several of the leaves were written in pencil, numerous remarks on the work, but as I consider them to have been the private observations of Captain Bligh, and written unsuspecting the much lamented event which subsequently took place, they shall by me be held sacred.

If the outline I have here given has not been adequate to the reader's expectation, I trust the short period in which I had to collect the materials, will, in some degree, plead my apology; under which impression I shall leave Pitcairn's Island, but not without a hope that its interesting inhabitants will receive that support from this country, the peculiarity of their situation so justly entitle them to, and proceed to Valparaiso, where we arrived after a voyage of 30 days, when we had neither bread in our lockers, nor wine in our casks; therefore, the reader will not be surprised, if, while he rests, that I should indulge myself with a few of the luxuries of the Port.

o

CHAPTER VI.

The reader will be aware that the period afforded me at our first arrival in this port, was inadequate to furnish sufficient materials for a correct description, either of its importance or situation, and will not only attribute any silence to so obvious a reason, but permit me here to make it the theme of a short chapter.

Valparaiso then may be considered as one of the most commodious, opulent, and extensive Ports on the coast of Chili, and is situated in latitude 33° 1′ south, and in longitude 72° 19′ west, at about ninety miles from the city of Santiago, the capital of the country. This town being divided into two parts, and known by the names of the Port Valparaiso, and the Almendrale, I shall to prevent confusion speak of them separately. The Port is, doubtless, the most ancient, and from its being the immediate mart for every kind of merchandize in the country, it is of the greatest consideration. The town is built as regular as the ground on which it stands will allow, and possesses two or three tolerable streets; the rest, and which is by far the greatest part, occupies the sides and summits of those heights, which run with great abruptness even to the beach. Through each of those streets cross several zig-zag roads and smaller paths, leading from them to the different dwellings. The houses, with a few exceptions (as throughout the country) are but one story, and built of large unburnt bricks, have rather a mean appearance, and those situated on the beach are occupied by merchants, either as magazines for corn, or ships; and where the principal port of their commercial affair is transacted. The chief article of commerce consists in corn, cordage, and copper; the two first being brought from the neighbouring fertile valley of Quillota; the last from beyond St. Jago.

The custom House, with all its establishment, is on the beach, and all boats (His British Majesty's excepted) are obliged to land there. Both officers and men belonging to this department appear to be vigilant in their stations, and steady in the performance of their duty; but I believe, from the Governor to the lowest individual in the establishment, there are few who can withstand the temptation of a "cohecho de oro," or a bribe of gold.

There are two churches but neither worthy

of notice, and monasteries or convents there are none.

In the centre of the town, and commanding it in either direction, is situated the citadel, consisting of a small battery of 12 guns towards the sea, and a wall surrounding an inconsiderable piece of ground, in which is the Governor's residence and prison. This place bears not the least resemblance to a regular fortification, and the rivers described by Frozier to run on either side, must have been from fancy alone. I sought for them, but in vain; however, there are certainly channels, and in the rainy season they may contain a considerable quantity of water—at any other period certainly not. There is a deep well in the garrison, and another greatly within the range of its cannon. The whole is in the greatest possible state of disorganization, but let it be in never so fine a state, it is not tenable against any force which may be in possession of the heights above, for as the mountain is steep, the citadel becomes soon exposed; insomuch, that at the distance of half a gun shot, it is quite open and unprotected.

Castello Blanco, or the White Castle, stands on the beach immediately under a high cliff, at the west point of the bay, flanking the harbour to the eastward. It mounts but 8 cannons, is wholly unprotected from the land, and capable of little resistance from the sea, as a ship of any force going against it, the garrison would not long be able to stand at their guns.

The anchorage here is very good, but the most secure and protected is towards the White Castle, the opposite side being a shoal as well as having some dangerous rocks, which are at no period visible above the surface of the water. The shore from the citadel to below the Custom House is very bold, and ships of considerable burden can anchor within a few yards of the beach, so that they can conveniently take in, or discharge the cargoes.

It is impossible for ships of force to be supplied, at any time, with water from the port without incalculabe trouble, for it is in the rainy season alone that there is any, but what is contained in the wells; however, at the Almendrale it may be procured at all seasons, when the surf will permit the boats to land, as I shall hereafter mention.

All kind of trading with this country being prohibited by the Spanish Government, the quantity of European goods imported here is but trifling, and of a most exhanced price; but great smuggling is now carried on across the Cordilliras, and all sorts of contraband goods are introduced by the British residents at Buenos Ayres, and their agents. The immediate produce of the country is confined to corn, hemp, and cordage, which are brought here in great quantities, and shipped for Lima, and the different ports of Peru; and as that country is nearly as deftitute of these articles as Chili is of sugar, coffee, &c. &c. these are their principal goods brought back in exchange. In fact, these two countries appear dependent on each other; and without a friendly underftanding, and which is so much to the intereft of both to have, they muft be equally distreffed. During the Patre, or revolution in Chili, corn in Peru was at 12 and 14 dollars the English single bufhel, while sugar and coffee, in Chili, was at 6s. 6d. or 7 fhillings the pound.

I muft not omit to mention the market, which, with the governor's house, forms a square, and is abundantly supplied with every article of subsistence, particularly poultry, vegetables, and fruit, whose prices are very moderate, Notwithstanding the apple is at all times so plentiful, and so superior in quality, they have not as yet began to make cider. The grapes also are of unequalled quality, but the wine is seldom drinkable. The peach, apricot, and nectarine, are in their seasons extremely large and of a most delicious flavour. The frutillia, or strawberry, although in size equal to three or four of ours, is by no means so agreeable to the taste.

This country is abundantly supplied with every species of cattle, and an ox weighing about 400 lbs. (which is the common size) may be procured for 10 or 12 dollars. The horses are not large, but finely formed, fleet, and spirited; and when trained, are so tender in the mouth, that the most trivial touch of the rein is sufficient when going full speed to stop them in an instant—a sharp check, on the spot, if the rider be not on his guard, it is no more than probable that he will be precipitated over his head, which was a frequent occurrence with the sailors when on their equestrian excursions.

The population of the port, joined to that of the Almendrale, is computed by the Spaniards to be nearly 20,000, but I have no conception it can be so many by nearly a third.

A mountain whose abrupt termination leaves only sufficient room for a narrow road between it and the beach, separates the port of Valparaiso and the Almendrale, or Almond Grove, at the distance of 300 yards; but even in this space there are a few hovels formed in the rock, so it may literally be said there is a direct line of communication from the one to the other.

This place is built on a plain of more than a mile in length, and half as much in width, and consists of one long street running directly through it, with smaller ones leading to the right and left. It is said to contain upwards of 5000 people—has several small churches, and one small monastery. It is so great a mart for fruit, that at almost every door there are various sorts exhibited for sale. Several gardens of great extent are occupied by almond trees, from which the place derives its name. There are also large vineyards, in one of which, situated about the centre of the town, is the well from whence the shipping are supplied with water. In is drawn in buckets by means of a wheel, and is sufficient to keep in continual supply 3 or 4 large oses, or pipes. The greatest inconvenience is the distance, (400 or 500 yards,) to roll the caſks, they muſt also be rafted off, as there is at all times too great a surf to get them easily into boats.

At the end of this town commences the grand road to the city, made by O'Higgins during his presidentship. A guard is always kept there, and all travellers muſt have their passports backed by the offices, or at Casa Blanca (12 leagues distant) he will be prevented from proceeding on his journey. The temperature here is generally moderate, and the country healthy. The thermometer from 68° to 73°.

During the months of June, July, August, and September, it is continual rain, and is very properly called the rainy season. In the other months there is seldom a cloud, and except a fog in the morning, it is always serene. The country for several miles round, is nothing but steril mountains, scorched by the sun in the summer, or deluged by the rain in the winter; however, the vallies in the interior are very beautiful, and among them Quillota may be considered not only the most extensive, but fertile. The town, from which it takes its name, lies about 30 miles in a N. E. direction from Valparaiso, and the road leading to it for some distance is rugged, and the country barren. By this route, you pass the small bay where the American Frigate Essex was captured by the Phœbe and Cherub, and where many of her crew swam on shore, and as many perifhed in the attempt. Paffing this place, and ascending an eminence, the principal part of the port opens itself to view, and with it the traveller cannot but be gratified, for notwithftanding

P

the ſterility of the mountains, want of cultivation, trees, &c. there is a certain ſtrangeness in the appearance, which excited in me considerable interest. Advanced thus far, the valley and town of Quillota appear in front, whose lively aspect when compared with the country you have passed over, forms a very striking contrast. Quillota is most abundantly supplied with every description of fruit, and the only attention paid the trees, is causing the trenches in which they are planted to be kept constantly moist throughout the dry season. This fertile valley is also productive of corn, hemp, and cordage, of the finest qualities, which is generally transported on mules to Valparaiso, either for the purpose of being shipped or mauufactured The rope when made, contains nothing but the hemp in its natural state, as the tar of the country is of too destructive a nature to be mixed with it, and that of Europe too expensive to be brought for that purpose. The riches of this valley, are not confined alone to the fertility of its surface; the earth for several feet deep, contains a portion of gold, which is, when waſhed, of great purity. The silver mines likewise are very rich. It was here, and in consequence of its abounding in gold, that the Spaniards under Peter de Baldivia erected a fort for the security of the settlement, and to keep in awe those Indians whom he employed to bring him treasure. "But," says Frazier, "they poſſeſſed themselves of it by a very ingenious stratagem. One of those, on an appointed day, carried thither a pot full of gold dust, to excite the curiosity of the garrison soldiers. In a short time they all gathered about that little treasure, and whilst they were busy contending their private interests, to divide the same, an ambuscade of Indians concealed and armed with arrows, rushed in upon them, and found them defenceless. The victors then destroyed the fort, which has never been rebuilt since, and they gave over searching for gold there." I was not at the town, but am informed by a gentleman who had been there, it is very inconsiderable—principally inhabited by the natives of the country, and not containing more than a hundred families that are white. Mules are the only animals used, to transport their goods from one place to another, and consequently great numbers must be daily employed; in some of the teams I have seen upwards of three hundred. They travel with great celerity, and if it be more than one day's journey, they are unloaded and their burdens formed into an encampment. If the traveller chuses, he may return from the valley of Quillota to the port by another route, but before he reaches the Camino Real, or royal road, he will find it exceedingly rugged and disagreeable.

In the south-east direction, and about ten miles from Valparaiso, is the Lagoon, on which there is frequently good shooting. Swans are found there, and at times black ones. There are also, near this place, some very good farms.

The natives of Chili are very expert at throwing the *Lesso*, and by which every kind of animal is caught. The process is thus. A man with a rope of 20 yards or upwards in length (having at the end to be delivered, a noose) coiled in his right hand, turns it twice, or thrice over his head to create velocity 'ere he throws it at the object, which, let it be a bull, never so wild, he will be sure to take him by the horns or head. They are so exceedingly dexterous at this work, that they will, with the same facility, take a bullock by the leg, as they can by the head or neck.

When speaking of the garrison, I omitted to say the Governor is also military commandant, and has under him about 700 men, who are natives of the country, badly dressed, undisciplined, and I believe generally disaffected to the Spanish Government. It is hardly poſſible to impress the reader with a proper idea of their dress or arms ; but a guard, when turned out, is the most motley group I ever beheld or could have imagined. Among a score it may be confidered extraordinary, if there can be found one pair of shoes or stockings. Their arms also, are very defective.

It may not be improper, if I here, by way of conclusion to this chapter, make a fhort digreffion, and give an outline of what paffed in this country subsequent to our first arrival in the port, when we found Capt. Hellier, of the Phœbe, had juft returned from Chilan, after having succeeded in concluding a treaty with the Patriots for an armistice of one year, during which period, the country was to enjoy a free trade, and the Spanish flag to be refpected. By this treaty, and which I have underftood he was authorized to make by the Viceroy of Lima, on any terms, the Spanifh army under Gen.. Gança, was extricated from that fate which otherwise awaited it. The prisoners alfo, and among whom were officers of talents and diftinction, were set at liberty, and conveyed by us, as I have before ftated, to Lima. This object effected, which was the end of the Viceroy's views, he broke the treaty entered into on his part by Capt. Hellier, under a pretence that he had exceeded his inftructions, and began immediately to prepare a fresh expedition against Chili, and the arrival of the Talavera Regiment from Spain, which thirsted for rapine and plunder, enabled him to carry his wishes into instant effect. This expedition, Ossorio, a Spaniard by birth, and I understand possessed of all the bad qualities inherent in his countrymen, without a single good one of his own, was appointed to command. Every thing to facilitate his complemention was done, but, however much the viceroy might have wished to prevent it, the news soon reached Chili, and in the interim, measures were taken in that country to counteract his duplicity. But those who had been in opposition to Capt. Hellier's convention, instead of uniting with them, upbraided his party with treachery, and of having sold their country. These reproaches however justly they might have been applied, were sharpened by other invectives, and at length their private resentment preponderating against the public good, hostilities commenced between the two parties; the Carrares heading one, the Roses the other. During the internal broils, and battles which followed, the common enemy to both was wholly lost sight of, and they placed themselves on the margin of that precipice from which they were ultimately hurled. Ossorio's expedition had been completed, sailed, and arrived at Conception ; nay, he was even on his march towards Kancagua before their unnatural delirium was at all dispatched. When he arrived, he found his forces greatly inferior in number to what he had to contend with, but relying on the superior discipline of the Talavara regiment, he was anxious to bring them to battle, as the Chilinans were disunited amonst themselves, and destitute even of a chief or officer, on whom they could place confidence for either abilities, or courage. A battle soon ensued, and wonderful to relate, the Chilinans fought so determinedly, that for a confiderable time the day was doubtful, and it is said that had young Carrares joined with his regiment, instead of standing aloof at this critical moment, the Spaniards would have been obliged to retreat ; but be this as it may, the battle was lost, the Patriots leaving on the field more than 1000 in killed and wounded. Kancagua was taken immediate possession of, the Patriots dispersed, and the Carrares with their regiment plundered the churches, and levying contributions, croffed the Cordilleras, and reached Mendoza in safety, with booty to an immense amount, leaving theunhappy country to her fate. St Jago, the Capital, inftead of making resistance, erected triumphal arches for the victor, and strewed flowers before him as he entered. Thus was a country, which, for four years had breathed the pure air of liberty and freedom, subjugated, and they may, with great propriety, date the epoch of their new slavery, from the period of their inconsiderate treaty of Chilan.

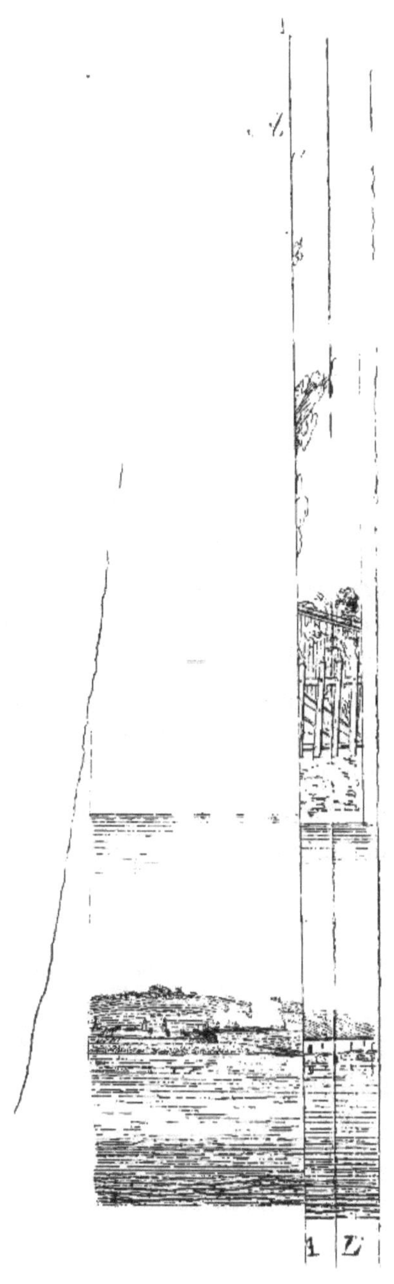

CHAPTER VII.

The time now elapsed subsequent to arriving in Port, had fully compensated for our sufferings during our voyage from the Marquesas, and as the ship had also undergone a tolerable refit, we sailed for the port of Callao, where we arrived after touching at Coquimbo, and experiencing the finest weather, on the fifth day.

Callao, the port of Lima, stands on a low narrow neck of land, near the ruins of the old town, and almost level with the sea. This Isthmus, for it can be termed nothing else, with the Island of San Lorensa forms the anchorage, which is one of the most spacious, and beautiful in the world; and as the wind is never tempestuous or strong, excepting when indicative of an Earthquake, ships may anchor, or moor in the greatest safety with a rope or hawser of comparatively small size. The Jutty, or landing place, is formed by a ship which was run on shore for that purpose, so that the surf being completely broken, boats are at all times enabled to land, and lie then, with as much security as if in a still

Q

View of CALLAO

pond. To this place there are several streams of water brought for the conveniency of ships, which can always be supplied with the greatest expedition.

The present town of Callao, does not amount to more than 300 houses, which are, like those of Paita, built of bamboo and mud; they are equally mean in their appearance, and from the number of sailors which are constantly here, the greater part of them are occupied for public houses, or shops retailing *Agua dent* or spirit of the country.

The custom house is situated at a little distance from the jutty—it is an extensive establishment, and, like those at Valparaiso, all departments are ready to sacrifice the public good, or rather the good of the state, to gratify their own insatiable thirst for riches. It has a governor and a numerous train of satellites. The trade carried on here is considerable from the different countries of Mexico, Quito, and Chili; from whence they are supplied with pitch, tar, and sulphur, with wines, spirits, wood, cocoa, and Guayaquil hats.—Corn, hemp, cordage, hides, &c. &c. are generally imported from Chili, and from the Island of Chiloe the woolen manufactures of the natives, such as the poncho, and rugs; some of the latter are curious from the strange figures represented, and are generally ufed as carpets for the ladies to reft their feet on. Sugar, coffee, chocolate, and peruvian bark, are the principal articles exported. For the protection of the roadftead there are thiee batteries, one of which is of great extent and ftrong. In the centre is a chapel, the refidence of the Governor, and soldiers' barracks: and under the baftions, which are bomb proof, is fufficient room to contain the pricipal part of the Spaniards, or people to the number of 6 or 7000. The fmaller ones are at a fmall diftance to the North, and South, each forming a crefcent projecting to the sea, and mounting in *barbet* six long pieces of ordnance.

The importance of thefe batteries, as a defence, or guard for Lima is but little, for fhipping may anchor, and troops land much out of the range of fhot from their longeft pieces; and as the wells of the garrifon contain nothing but water, too brackifh for long, or conftant ufe, their prefent fupply, which is brought in a canal from the river Lima, can be inftantly ftopped, which must inevitably reduce it in a fhort period. I understood they had tried every method, but in vain, to prevent fea water from penetrating, and are about to make frefh attempts; but, in my opinion, if I may judge from the local situation of the place it will be as fruitless as their former ones, for the isthmus is narrow, and the ground where it stands is the ruins of ancient Callao, which was about the year 1740 swallowed by one of those terrible convulsions of nature, so common in that country. The old ruins to a great extent are quite viſible, inſomuch that ſeveral of the arches of different churches are now above the surface. They appear to have gone down bodily, and but little out of perpendicular; the one under which I went, ſtood perfectly erect.

In digging the trenches of the batteries, many thousand sculls have been taken up, which are, with other bones, continually carried under the roofs of theſe once splendid sanctuaries, and there deposited. The country near Callao is very level, and the earth contains such an abundance of nitre, that at many places the ground is covered with great quantities naturally chryſtalized; there is a great deal made in the neighbourhood, but particularly at Lima. The village of Bella Viſta, or Belle View, ſtands in a pretty ſituation, and is an agreeable walk in the cool of the evening from the Port. The road leading to Lima is very commodious and ſtraight, has a wall of mud on each ſide, and the city, which is ſeven miles from the port, being only 300 feet above the sea, the ascent is hardly perceptible; on the contrary, there is so great a deception, that either going to, or coming from, it has the appearance of a descent.

At about four miles on the road, trees have been planted on each ſide, which, with the gardens being conſtantly in bloom for some fruit or other, makes the entrance into Lima peculiarly delightful.

For the space of two miles from the gates there are alſo walks with ſeats on either ſide, at convenient diſtances, for the accommodation of the public, and during the evening they are generally frequented by the faſhionable part of the inhabitants, either in their calaſhes or coaches, or on foot.

By this road then, and under a large, but not very magnificent archway, you enter the city of Lima, celebrated for its great riches, and having had one of its ſtreets paved with ingots of silver, as well as having for its founder the great Franciſco Pizzero, who it seems caused it to be begun, either in the year of our Lord 1534, or 1535. It is, like moſt of the other towns founded by the Spaniards, laid out in squares of 150 yards each way, with streets of a proportional width, crossing each other at right angles. Those running from East to West, have a conſtant ſtream of water, and as the descent is sufficient, all the dirt, which, otherwise would be offenfive, is carried off. Those going from North to South do not poffess this advantage. In this city, it being the Spanish Capital of the Peruvian dominions, is the residence of the Viceroy, who may in every sense be considered as an absolute monarch.

The Prefident of Chili is subservient to him, but from the diftance which separates them, he is precluded from having much controul over his actions. The Marquis of Concordia was then the Viceroy of Peru, and Offorio, the Prefident of Chili.

The extent of this city may be estimated to be nearly eight miles in circumference, including the suburb on the north fide of the river, or about 2 miles 3 quarters in length, and a mile and half in width. Its fortification confifts, merely of a wall built of unburnt bricks, from 15 to 20 feet high, and nearly as many thick, with baftions flanking each other at a diftance not exceeding two hundred yards.

The width of the breaft work from the infide extremity of the parapet, is by no means adequate to permit the mounting of cannon, and it appears evident to have been intended only to protect the city from the incurfions of, or being surprized by the Indians.

According to Frazier, whose plan, as well as description of the place, I found to be exceedingly correct, it was built in 1685 by John Ramond a Flemish Priest in the Viceroyship of the Duke de la Plata.

It is now very neglected, and out of repair, but the disaffected state of the country seems to have created some just alarm among the Spaniards, and the Marquis of Concordia has ordered several gateways to be repaired, and the wall to be put in a proper state of defence; but its great state of disorganization precludes its being accomplished in any reasonable time. It possesses no kind of ditch, or out-works.

At about 150 yards, or one square from the bridge, is the Placa Real, or Royal Square, in the centre of which are the remains of an elegant brass fountain; several of the lions with which it was embellished, as well as part of the statue of Fame still remain. The water is thrown to a considerable height, and the basin is sufficiently spacious for it to fall within its margin. On the east side of this square is the the cathedral, and palace of the bishop. The Viceroy's establishment occupies the North side; the West is taken up by the court of justice, council house, and prison, with a row of arches, which are continued throughout the South side, and under them are shops of various descriptions. There is a market held in this square, but it cannot boast of any particular excellence.

The Cathedral does not poſſess any external beauty ; but the splendour, magnificence, and riches of the interior can alone be conceived. The enchanted palaces as described in the fairy tales, recurred to my memory the inſtant I entered this elegant ſanctuary. The great altar, ſtanding at the Eaſt-end, is modern, and the columns numerous as they are, together with every other part, are covered with silver in about the thickness of a dollar, and when lit up, for the performance of any particular ceremony, its brilliant and beautiful appearance cannot be exceeded. Don Mathias Maſtro, a Prieſt, was the architect. He is also a painter of considerable merit. The various altars on either side, are equal in richness if not in beauty, to the one I have mentioned. The Church of San Auguſtin may be considered the next in beauty, by many I dare say superior to the Cathedral ; all the altars are superbly ornamented, and several are of incalculable value, but particularly the one, erected at the entire expence of the Silversmiths, which is covered with solid metal, of more than common thickness, it only required a few additional ornaments which were in a ſtate of readiness, to make it complete.

This church contains some excellent paintings. San Domingo also vies with the others in point of elegance, and has a handsome tower, of great height, at the top of which the traveller may enjoy a moſt extensive, picturesque, and intereſting proſpect; and as it is difficult for a ſtranger to find his way through the town, I would recommend him to visit this tower the firſt thing, as, from a single look he will receive more information relative to the place, than from studying the Lima directory a month.

As the city contains upwards of fifty Churches, and Chapels, the reader will see, the impoſſibility of my bringing all before him, and consider it sufficient, if, in addition to those I have already mentioned, I say that San Francisco with with La Conception, and La Mercy are the moſt extensive, as well as handsome; although none of the others are in the leaſt deficient in riches, and splendor.

The monaſteries here, are both numerous and spacious, and I should suppose of the different orders there cannot be less than eighteen or twenty, and some among them contain three or four squares, or a piece of ground equal at leaſt to six acres.

The largeſt of those is, of the Franciscan order, and contains from 1200 to 1500 Friars. The Auguſtins come next, and I think the

R

monaftery itfelf, although not fo large, is much more elegant than the former; the number of monks exceed a thousand. These have two or three fmaller ones in different parts of the city. There are also numerous eftablifhments of this nature under the various denominations of Dominicans, Benedictines, Mercerarians, &c. &c. and are generally found in the moft defirable and advantageous situations.

Of convents for nuns, there are alfo feveral, and of great extent: but those of St. Clare, the Carmelites, and the Incarnation are the principal ones of note.

The number of men wearing the monaftic habit, I was affured exceeded 10,000, and of women nearly 6,000, which may be confidered nearly one sixth of the population of the place. Besides the monks, there are a numerous train of Clerigos, a fort of parifh Priefts, who, with the former poffess a life of celibacy, but, if detected in any frailties of nature, their punifhment is not fo exemplary; their oaths being only against matrimony.

It may be imagined perhaps, in a place, where the holy minifters of religion are so numerous—where sanctuaries for its performance are so splendid, that piety and devotion would be predominant features, but the most depraved heart is often concealed under this specious covering, and I am fully justified in saying that it is no where more so than here; for the cloisters of both sexes, with a few exceptions, instead of being the sacred habitation of piety, abstinence, and resignation, is that of riotous living, debauchery, libertinism, and licentiousness. Some of the Friars even boast of their manifold conquests, and numerous progeny; and in many instances, even that small semblance of religion which they assume occasionally, is entirely shaken off. "The penitent women" says Frazier "have also a place of retreat, but I do think not it very full, because of the little scruple, they make in that country of libertinism, and the little care that is taken to curb it."

He could not have come to a more just conclusion, and as there appears to have been but little reform, if any at all, in their moral lives subsequent to that period, we may be led to suppose that there are at present many vacancies in this establishment, which is known by the name of las Amparadas de la Conception, or the protected of the Conception.

In the university of this place, there are several colleges, formed on very liberal principles, but now much neglected. Formerly they contain or had attached to them, more than 150 professors of Divinity, Law, Physic, and Philosophy, and feveral thousand ftudents were inftructed in every branch of literature, but at prefent the number of teachers as well as scholars are considerably reduced, and science (if there was ever any there) feems to have wholly deferted the walls, for with the exception of Latin, and a little divinity, there is nothing taught.

The asylum for Lunatics in this city, is very extensive and supported by voluntary contributions. It was exceedingly full when I went over it, and every possible attention appeared to be paid to the comfort of the patients.

The Viceroy is at the head of the Royal Court, and, if he choses, may preside, but this seldom occurs, except in matters of the greateft importance, and where the safety of the ftate may be affected.

Sixteen Judges, four Magiftrates, two Attorney Generals, and two or three others of less note, making in all 25 or 26, form this August Tribunal, which with the exception of the Seraphic Inquisition, is paramount to all others. Subservient to this, there are several other courts, such as the Court of Juftice, Criminal Court, Exchequer, Chancery, &c. There is alfo a Mayor, and Aldermen, who have a Court for the punifhment of offences within their jurisdiction, and not cognisable by the others. It will be needless for me to say that where Priestcraft has taken so deep root, there are spiritual Courts in abundance; but the most grievous, as well as terrific, is the Inquisition, against whose decision there is no appeal, and from whose prisons no one, let him be never so innocent, is safe. The accused is always kept in ignorance of his accuser, nor has he the privilege allowed him of confronting any of the witnesses, which may suborned against him.

Many of the Priests who are in favor of this detestable establishment, would fain persuade you that its abolition was productive of a regret in the public mind, which its re-establishment alone has been able to allay: but from what I could learn, I am impressed with a very different opinion, and I think the conduct demonstrated by the mob, when the Viceroy withheld the order for the entire suspensions of its functions, is sufficient to bear me out. The Marquis of Concordia had received such orders from the Cortes of Spain, but being himself a favorite of the institution he withheld putting it in force for nearly six months, and also strove to conceal that such orders had really arrived; however, it at length became known, when the public being no longer able to smother their indignation, joined in one furious mob, burſt open the gates, and not regarding even their immediate saints, demoliſhed every ensign of Inquisitorial power. The Council Chamber was deſtroyed—the Images broken—their records thrown in the ſtreets—the secret prisons were explored, the innocent immured therein set at liberty; and perhaps, had the officers of this seraphic and illustrious order been present, they would have experienced that puniſhment which was inflicted on the emblems of their tyranny.

Thus much was related to me by a gentleman who was conspicuous in the affair, and willing to possess himself of their records, he broke open a desk, which luckily contained what he wanted. These proved to be manuscript trials, confeſſions, and allegations, but when the order came for the re-establishment of this tribunal, he, dreading lest these documents might be found upon him, destroyed the greatest part, and was about to set fire to the last bundle, when I entered his room. I saw they were old manuscripts, and without aſking their contents, or crime they had committed, risqued them from their impending danger, and have them now in my poſſeſſion. They contain chiefly allegations againſt the

Friars for libertinism, and immorality, and even of offering violence to women to whom they have been called as spiritual confessors.

The Inquisition is situate at the east part of the city, and occupies more than one square. It has three entrances, but the most considerable one is in the centre, the others being chiefly attached to the residences of its principal officers. The Council Chamber must have been a superb room, and the offices attached to it have the appearance of having been once splendid. Behind these, come the *carceles secretos*, or the secret prisons, which are infinitely more miserable than the others are elegant. Each of these gloomy dungeons, where so many innocent persons have lingered a life of pain, and wretchedness, and of whose fate their friends have been ignorant, is about 8 or 10 feet square, and nearly 20 feet high, having at the top a small door, admitting as small a portion of light as air, and which is not at their own disposal, nor can they enjoy it, but at the caprice of those in whose charge they are, and is at no period more than sufficient for them to discern some figure of torment which may be on the wall, for the purpose of putting the unhappy victim in mind of death or a frightful futurity.

The different Courts of Inquisition bearing

so nice affinity to each other, in their arrangements, mode of procedure, &c. that I cannot here resiſt offering to the notice of the reader a few abridged extracts from Monsieur Dellon, and I hope they will not not prove uninteresting.

"During the months of November and December, I heard every morning the ſhrieks of the unfortunate victims, who were undergoing the Queſtion.* The Auto da feé, as I

---

* The Question evidently appears to be the *Torture*, of which there are three different sorts, and the first being the most exquisite, is called the Queen of Torture. The criminal's hands being tied behind his back, and fastened to a rope, which, by means of four cords drawn over pullies at each corner of a lofty room, he is hoisted up to the ceiling in an instant, when he is again let down within a few inches of the ground. This is thrice repeated, and by the sudden jirks all his bones are dislocated. In this state he hangs until he expires, or confesses.

2d. Torture.—The instrument is something like a smith's anvil, with a spike not very sharp at the top. Ropes as in the former instance, are from the corners of the room attached to the criminal's legs and arms; he is drawn up a little, and is then let down with his back bone exactly upon the spike of iron where the whole of his weight rests.

3d. Torture.—Is what they term a slight Torture, and applied only to women. Matches of tow and pitch are wrapped round their hands, and set on fire until the flesh is consumed.——See Mr. Bower's account of the Inquisition at Maccrata.

remember to have heard, was generally celebrated on the first Sunday in Advent, because the service read on that day is part of the Gospel, touching on the last judgment, and the Inquisitors pretend by this ceremony to exhibit a lively emblem of that awful event. The profound silence within the walls enabled me to count the number of doors open at the time of meals, and I was convinced of there being many prisoners. Advent passed, and I prepared myself to pass another year in melancholy captivity. On the 11th Jan. I was aroused from my despair. My prison door was opened, the Alciade presented me with a habit, and left me with a light in my dungeon. The guard came about two o'clock, and led me into a long gallery, where I found the companions of my fate ranged against the wall, and had it not been for the movement of the eyes, they would have resembled ſtatues rather than animated beings. I was placed amongſt this melancholy band; those condemned to be burnt, were with their confessors in another part of the room—the women were in a room adjoining—we here received a large wax candle, and a yellow dress, with the cross of Saint Andrew, painted before and behind; it is called the San Benito. To relapsed heretics the Samarra was given, the colour of which was

S

grey, and on it was was painted the portrait of the sufferer surrounded with torches, flames, and devils. The Carrochas, or caps of pastboard, of a conical ſhape, covered with demons and fire, was then presented them. It was about sun-rise when the great bell of the Cathedral announced to the people of Goa the auguſt ceremony of the Auto da Feé, and we were led from the gallery into the great hall, one by one, and there given in charge of Parrains or godfathers, who were to guard us to the place of execution. With them we went forth to the street, where I saw that the proceſſion commenced by Dominican Friars, in honour to San Dominic, the founder of the Holy Tribunal. As I was not one of the leaſt guilty, I did not go foremost—we walked bear-footed through the ſtreets, and the ſharp ſtones wounded my tender feet dreadfully, and caused the blood to ſtream. The crowd of spectators was innumerable. Arrived at the church of St. Francis, the Inquisitor and Counsel were on one ſide the altar, the Viceroy, and Court on the other. The prisoners were now seated, and an Auguſtin Monk mounted the pulpit, and preached for half an hour, and I could not help noticing the comparison he drew between the Inquisition and Noah's Ark, in which he made this diſtinction, that the creatures which entered the Ark, left it on the cessation of the deluge with their original properties, whereas the Inquisition had this singular characteristic, that those who came within its walls, cruel as wolves, and fierce as lions, went forth gentle as lambs. The sentences were next read, and my joy at hearing I was not to be burnt, but serve in the gallies, was extreme. The Priest, with a wand, gave me in turn a stroke on the breast and released me from excommunication. Here I cannot resist mentioning a circumstance which will shew their excessive superstition in matters relating to the Inquisition. During the procession the person who was my godfather (though I frequently addressed him) would not speak to me, and even refused me a pinch of snuff, so apprehensive was he that in so doing he should participate in the censure under which he conceived me to lie; but the moment I was absolved, he embraced me, presented me his snuff box, and told me that thenceforth he should consider me as a brother. The victims, destined to be immolated, were now brought forth, and receiving a blow upon the breast to signify they were abandoned, they were led away to the bank of the river where the Viceroy, and Court were assembled, and consigned to the faggots which had been previously prepared."

During the period I was employed in visiting this place, in which so many innocent beings have been the victims of the most remorseless tyranny; the emphatic words of Dr. Buchanan, in his Christian researches in Asia, recurred to my memory, and I pondered on the mysterious dispensation which permitted the Minifters of the Inquisition, with their racks, and flames, to visit these lands before the heralds of peace.

The mint is an eftablifhment of the greatest importance both to the ftate as well as to the individual. It is exceedingly extensive, and a very considerable number of men are continually employed, either immediately at the completion of the different coins, or separating the gold from the earth. This process is rather long, and effected by quicksilver. The silver is generally brought from the mines in flabs of about 120 to 220lbs weight, and the proportion of copper to one of the latter is 25lbs. which is added in melting.

The furnace in which this process takes place, is of clay, and the heat produced from charcoal, blown by a double pair of large bellows. When the metal is sufficiently united, it is run into moulds nearly a quarter of an inch deep, from whence it is conveyed to the machinery, which is of inferior powers, but passing through rollers, it is reduced to the required thickness, or so that the punch will cut out the exact weight of the coin to be produced.

After this, the edge is milled, when it is in a ſtate for taking the impreſſion, which is the finiſhing ſtroke, and is performed by means of a ſtamp, whose power appears to be similar to that of our modern printing preſſes. This department may be conſidered a Royalty of itself, as the governor is independent of the Viceroy within its walls, and can order the execution of any person without form, trial, or sanction, from another power. There are many clerks who have handsome salaries.

At the diſtance of a mile and a half in the Eastern direction of the city there is an extensive powder manufactory, and they boaſt of its producing the beſt article of this kind in the world, and I should not be surprized if it was so, because the whole of its ingredients are found here in great abundance, Near this place, is the Pantheon de los Meurtos, or the Pantheon of the dead, which has so handsome and lively appearance that a ſtranger would not be impressed with an idea of its being the sacred repository of those who are no more.

The river Limac, or Lima, is very inconsiderable, except in the season when the greatest proportion of snow melts. At all other periods, it is fordable, and at all places.

Crofling the bridge, which is not handsome, and continuing along the ftreet, you are led to the Almeada, or a public walk, so delightfully fhaded by groves of orange trees, that the rays of the sun are always broken, and the odour from the trees, at all times agreeable. It is most frequented on Sunday evenings, but wherever the Viceroy goes he is sure to take with him a fafhionable retinue as well as a concourse of the mobility.

On this side the river, is the Torus, or Amphitheatre, for the exhibition of the bull fights, and it is said to be sufficiently spacious to contain 20,000 people, and from the number I saw there, I have no reason to doubt it. This brutal amusement, so disgraceful to a civilized power, is here held in high eftimation, and is generally performed during the months of January, February, and March. The manner in which the poor animals are fought, are various, but, I will give as correct an outline of what I saw as I am able. The number of bulls torturedfor one day's amusement and gratification, is confined to a score. Those are placed the night preceding the fight in a house, or yard appropriated to that use, from whence they are taken separately, into a ſtall of grate work, with a door opening into the Theatre. In this place they undergo in their turn the cruel ordeal of being ornamented with fantastic articles of finery, sewn either to the ſkin, or tacked with small nails to the horns, squibs too of gunpowder are set off the inſtant the door opens when the infuriated creature, eager to be free from one torture ruſhes upon another, for it is generally aſſailed by a ſhower of darts, carrying with them crackers which explode on ſticking in the ſkin. In this wild ſtate it is attacked by a gladiator on horseback, who displays great agility in his evading the animal; others now advance, and after a few turns the attractive part of this fascinating amusement begins. These men are armed with long spears, and paſſing the bull, make a thruſt at the sinews of the neck, but the inſtrument oftener lodges before the ſhoulder, and it is not unfrequent to see the handles of seven or eight ſticking up before the ſhoulder, the blades having perforated the animal. In this ſtate, if it be what they call a good bull, it will continue to fight, until faint from the loss of blood, it drops, when ceasing to afford more amusement, it is dispatched and withdrawn from the Theatre. The next mode is by a gladiator on foot who carries a red flag, and is armed with a small sword, and which is by far the least cruel, for, if he be at all expert, the animal ceases to exist at a single blow. The Indian mode is peculiar to themselves, and not less barbarous than the first. They are armed with spears, and about six forming a line, march boldly towards the bull, who often stands at bay, and when irritated by the arrows before described, he plunges upon them, they open, and in passing he receives two or three weapons in the neck; with which he returns, and undergoing the same experiment several times is killed. These acts of cruelty are to the Limenans, the greatest treat that can be afforded. It is their "*feast of reason and their flow of soul.*" On one of the animals receiving a blow, which draws it from the object of its pursuit, or to cause it to stagger, or drop, the Theatre resounds with the most rapturous applauses; but there is one thing to be said,— they are impartial in bestowing it, for the plaudits, on the bull, if he maims, or even kills a man, are not less reiterated, than if, by a judicious blow, the gladiator had himself gained the prize.

But even where morality, which is the ground work of every other perfection, is in so little repute, it is still to be wondered at, that any of the human race (leaving civilization out of the queſtion) can be so deſtitute of humani-ty. It was the ladies who most excited my surprize, for with them those brutal shouts of approbation seemed to emanate; yet ſtrange to relate they seemed in every other reſpect, as far as I could perceive, good natured, facetious, and agreeable. The Theatre ſtands in the city; it is spacious, but not elegant, and the dancing, although not at all in unison with the feelings of Engliſh modeſty, is conſidered delightful.

There is nothing peculiar in the dress of the Limenans, excepting the morning or walking habit of the ladies, which at firſt has a ſtrange and disagreeable appearance, but when the eye becomes accuſtomed to it, this impression wears off, and what so many at firſt have thought disguſting, they have afterwards been reconciled to. This dress conſiſts of a kind of petticoat so nicely plaited, that it will ſtand upright, and a hood tied round the waiſt, but is sufficiently large to be brought over the head, which, with the exception of one eye, is entirely enveloped. Nothing can facilitate an intrigue more than this, because the husband may meet his wife, the lover his sweetheart, and yet be ignorant of the circumſtance.

The mountains immediately in the vicinity

T

of Lima are of little confideration, St. Chrifioval alone being worthy of notice. This mountain is high, and difficult of access, but ascended to the chapel, or hermitage on the summit, the view it affords both of the city, and country, even to the Andes, is truly beautiful.

The squares which compose the town are divided, and subdivided by houses built in squares, and which are generally of two ftories. Their walls are very thick, and from the bricks being long, unburnt, and composed of elaftic materials, they are calculated the better to withftand the violent fhocks of earthquakes, which prevail to a greater or less degree, about the months of December and January. The houses are built on the moft airy principle, are spacious, and handsome, but, from the brick floors, together with mats, and every other harbour for fleas, their residences are exceedingly uncomfortable to an Englifhman; nor has long habit caused the people themselves to be unsusceptible to the annoyance of these insects, for they are always prepared with a piece of fleecy cloth about 4 inches wide, twifted into little tags, and whenever they feel one tickling (which is very frequently) this trap is applied and often with great fuccess. They are not all scrupulous about catching these little tormentors, or putting them to death, let the company be never so numerous or splendid, nor do I believe by doing it they are conscious of any transgreſſion on the ſtrict rules of modesty. Most of the ladies understand the Piano and Psaltery, and all paſſionately fond of dancing. There are many dances peculiar to the several kingdoms of South America, as in Peru that of Chocolatte, and in Chili, la Balsa de Tierra. The former has much the greateſt portion of modeſty, and as well as the latter, is performed by two people only.

The population of Lima, consists of Spaniards, Creoles, native Indians, and African slaves, and in either their manners, or customs, there is nothing very peculiar, as the subordinate claſſes follow the faſhion most predominant among the Spaniards. Their hours of visiting, commence in the cool of the evening, and continue to a late hour in the night. The guests are refreſhed with ices, lemonade, and preserves; and amused with either singing, accompanied with the guittar or psaltery, or dancing, to which may be added the more faſhionable accomplishment of gambling. At their meals they have a prodigious number of dishes, and generally partake a small portion of each; a stranger therefore if he studies his own comfort should be careful not to dine entirely from the first or second course, for the importunity he will meet with, to partake of the several subsequent ones will be so repeated, as to constrain him to commence again, however much it may be against his inclination. Indeed they are very hospitable, and betray great anxiety to have the visits of strangers, and use every means to make that visit agreeable. The spirit of gallantry is no where carried to a greater extent than in Lima, and a man of the most advanced age, enters the list with the young, gay, and giddy. This is very conspicuous at their routes, and must be productive of considerable amusement to any stranger. Their entertainments, or galas are splendid, and arranged with great taste; in fact, there is such a degree of emulation and spirit of rivalry amongst the fair sex, that they study to eclipse one another in the beauty, magnificence, and profusion of their preparations. The supper having been removed, and nothing but the dessert, which is comprised of the choisest fruits, and confectionary in all its various forms and classes remaining, the party stand prepared for the attack, and at a given signal the work of devastation commences, when all is the most complete confusion. Pyramids torn to their foundation—Pagodas upset—Images broken, and in this extraordinary scramble, they are intent not on eating, but on collecting as great a portion as poſſible, which is secured either in pockets, handkerchiefs, or hats, and he who on the following day presents the greatest number of young ladies with a proper ſhare of the entertainment, is conſidered of the greatest gallantry; and I have seen the eyes of an old Don of eighty years of age, sparkle with the fire of satisfaction at displaying his booty, and contemplating the pleasure which awaited him in the morning, when his favorite mistreſſes would become the ſharers of his trophies.

Prior to the conquest of Peru by the Spaniards, the only animal which had been domeſticated, and used to carry a burden, was the lama, but ſince the introduction of horses, and mules, it has gradually been neglected, and is now only used by some of the lower Indians in the interior. The lama, in ſhape somewhat resembles the camel, but its hair, or wool is prodigiously long, and of a very fine texture. It is calculated to carry a burden not exceeding a hundred pounds, travels very ſtately at his own rate, and when tired, stops of his own accord, nor is it poſſible the guide or drivers can make it resume its journey until it has reſted sufficiently. In their wild ſtate they are exceedingly fleet, and inhabit the most mountainous and rocky places. The Guanaca is a species of the lama, smaller and but seldom used to carry a load. It is an inhabitant of the Andes, and is most plentiful in the kingdom of Chili. Like sheep, they do not poſſess upper teeth, and having a valve or aperture in the upper lip, they emit through it with considerable force, for their defence, when attacked or irritated, a slimy sour liquid.

Almost every kind of fruit is found here in the greateſt abundance, as well as perfection; but those held in the higheſt eſtimation are the granadellia, and cherymoya; the latter resembles the soursop of the West Indies both in appearance and taſte, but it certainly is much more delicious.

The temperature of Lima, or in fact the whole extent of the vast coaſt of South America, when compared to that of the same latitude either on the coast of Brazil or Africa, is exceedingly mild and temperate, the reason of which is so pleasingly described by the learned Dr. Robertson in his general history of America, that I cannot withhold from introducing the following quotation. "While the negro" says the historian "on the coast of Africa, is scorched with unremitting heat, the inhabitant of Peru breathes an air equally mild and temperate, and is perpetually shaded under a canopy of grey clouds, which intercept the fierce beams of the sun, without obstructing his friendly influence.* Along the eastern coast of America, the climate, though more similar to that of the torrid zone in other parts of the earth, is nevertheless considerably milder than in those countries of Asia and Africa, which lie in the same latitude. If from the southern tropic, we continue our progress to the extremity of the American continent, we meet with frozen seas, and countries horrid, barren, and scarcely habitable for cold, much sooner than in the North.

Various causes combine in rendering the climate of America so extremely different from that of the ancient continent. Though the utmost extent of America, towards the North, be not yet discovered, we know that it advances mnch nearer to the pole than either Europe or Asia. Both these have large seas to the North, which are open during part ot the year; and, even when covered with ice,

* Ulloa, the navigator, from whom the Historian takes his authority, is certainly incorrect, for the sun is only obscured by clouds, from the period of his entering his Southern Solstice, to the time of his quitting it, when, the clouds disperse, and the sky becomes visible and serene for the following six months. This I had an opportunity of observing myself.

the wind that blows over them is less intensely cold, than that which blows over land in the same high latitudes. But in America, the land stretches from the river St. Lawrence towards the pole, and spreads out immensely to the west. A chain of enormous mountains, covered with snow and ice, runs through all this dreary region. The wind in paſſing over such an extent of high and frozen land, becomes so impregnated with cold, that it acquires a piercing keenness, which it retains in its progress through warmer climates, and it is not entirely mitigated until it reaches the gulph of Mexico. Over all the continent of North America, a north-weſterly wind, and exceſſive cold are synonymous terms. Even in the most sultry weather, the moment that the wind veers to that quarter, its penetrating influence is felt in a transition from heat to cold, no less violent than sudden. To this powerful cause, we may ascribe the extraordinary dominion of cold, and its violent inroads into the Southern provinces in that part of the globe. Other causes, no less remarkable, diminish the active power of heat in those parts of the American continent which lie between the tropics. In all that portion of the globe, the wind blows in an invariable direction, from Eaſt to Weſt. As this wind holds its course across the ancient continent, it arrives at the countries which stretch along the western ſhores of Africa, inflamed with all the fiery particles which it hath collected from the sultry plains of Asia, and the burning sands in the African deserts. The coaſt of Africa is, accordingly, the region of the earth which feels the most fervent heat, and is exposed to the unmitigated ardour of the torrid zone. But this same wind which brings such an acceſſion of warmth to the countries lying between the river of Senegal, and Cafraria, traverses the Atlantic Ocean, before it reaches the American ſhore. It is cooled in its passage over this vast body of water, and is felt as a refreſhing gale along the coast of Brazil, and Guiana, rendering these countries, though among the warmest in America, temperate, when compared with those which lie opposite to them in Africa. As this wind advances in its course, across America, it meets with immense plains, covered with impenetrable foreſts, or occupied by large rivers, marshes, and ſtagnating waters, where it can recover no considerable degree of heat. At length it arrives at the Andes, which run from North to South through the whole continent. In paſſing over their elevated, and frozen summits, it is so thoroughly cooled, that the greater part of the

U

countries beyond them, hardly feel the ardour to which they seem exposed by their situation. In the other provinces of America, from Tierra Firme weſtward to the Mexican empire, the heat of the climate is tempered, in some places, by the elevation of the land above the sea, in others, by their extraordinary humidity, and in all, by the enormous mountains scattered over this tract. The islands of America, in the torrid zone, are either small, or mountainous, and are fanned alternately by refreſhing sea and land breezes."

For a considerable extent, along the coaſt of Peru, as well as some diſtance in the interior, they have no rain, or nothing more than a drizzle, or small mist, called by the Spaniards *niebling*. In fact, if they ſhould be visited with a phenomenon of this nature, their houses being of a nature so susceptible to it, it would probably be attended with serious consequences. The dews here are very heavy.

In taking a view of the mines and mineral productions of South America, Potosi, from its celebrity, seems to claim a just priority, not more, from its natural situation, than from the abundance of metal which has been extracted from it. The mines of Potosi are situated in a mountain resembling a sugar loaf, standing in a spacious plain, and at the bottom, about a league in circumference. Garullasso, the Hiſtorian, from whom I take this information, does not give the altitude of Mount Potosi, but leaves us to cenjecture what it may be from its summit (which is a quarter of a league round) being exceſſively cold and frequently covered with snow. From its bearing the Indian name of Puno, signifying a place uninhabitable from cold, we may conclude that the whole of this district, notwithſtanding its proximity to the equator, is of a frigid temperature. "The climate of Potosi" says an author whose name I cannot well recollect "is so cold, that the Spanish women could not lay in there, without running imminent risk of their lives."

This mine appears to have been first discovered by some Indian servants of the Spaniards, about 40 years after their entering that country, and at the period, when Gonzales Pizarro had in the neighbourhood, his *repartimento*, or colony of Indians. These people not being able to enjoy the unrestricted pleasures of their fortune, or conceal it long from their masters, discovered it to them. Subsequent to which period, it has not only been worked to a great extent, but has also caused a town of considerable population to be built in the neighbourhood, and is now known by the name of Potosi. The silver extracted from this mine, at present, is very inconsiderable, the mountain having been worked in so many places, that it is now quite exhausted.

The mines of Choco produce Platina.* Those of Carabaya, Kimani near La Paz, Nasca, and Tiavaya are the principal gold mines. Vilques, and Huancavilica are famous for their quicksilver. Those of Yauli, Uchumayo, Arequipa, and Cocctea produce the different ores in all their claffes of silver, copper, lead, iron, and cobalt; also those of antimony, arsenic, and magnesia. Neither of these mines are at present worked to any considerable extent, owing to the inferiority of their machinery, but they were in daily expectation of engines, from England, when their works would again be resumed.

The cities, or towns of most consideration in the kingdom of Peru, are Cuzco, Arequipa, Huancavilica, Truxillo, Tarma. It will be

* M. Von Humbold has recently presented to the King of Prussia's Cabinet of minerals, the only lump of native platina that is known. He obtained it in 1800 in the soap manufactories of the town of Todda, in the province of Choco, in South America. This ingot is of the size of a pigeon's egg, and its absolute weight is 10,386 grains, and its specific weight 10,037 grains.

hardly necessary to inform the reader, that the former of these is the most ancient, or that it had for its founder, Manco Capac, or the first Inca. This city has been subsequently the royal residence of eleven of his illustrious race, when Atuhuallpa, or the twelfth Inca, usurped the throne, and after having been guilty of the most atrocious murders, and cruelties, on the legitimate descendants, lost his own dominions, and was himself strangled by the Spaniards under Pizarro. The no less strange than incestuous custom of keeping the royal blood pure, by marrying the presumptive heir to the throne, to his eldest sister, appears to have been continued, even to the latest periods of their sovereignty, or to the time of the revolution of Atuhuallpa. Huana Capac, the last Inca, and father of Huascar, and Atuhuallpa, married first his eldeſt ſiſter, who proving barren, married his second or youngest, Rava Oclla, by whom he had Huascar, the legitimate heir to the throne. Atuhuallpa was by the daughter of the King of Quito, whom he had conquered, and was considered illegitimate.*

Manco Capac, in his distribution of the ci-

* See Garcillazo de la Vegas Commentaries, Vol. I. page 275.

ty of Cuzco, displayed great talents, for few seem to be laid out to greater advantage. The Royal Palace, the Temple of the Sun, the offices of state, and houses belonging to the principal subjects, occupied an eminence, and received the name of Hanaun Cuzco, or Cuzco upon the hill, the remaining part being situated in the plain, is called Huin Cuzco. By the road of Antisuya the city is divided, and the minor divisions though numerous, are regular, for as the Inca reduced the savage people, which then inhabited the country, to his subjection, so he placed those he brought with him to the city, in the direction such conquest lay. Thus if the conquered came from the east, in an easterly direction from this Palace, a place was appropriated for their establishment, if from the west, in the west, and so on. Their immediate governor was taken or appointed from amongst them, and they were allowed to enjoy the customs used in their different countries. "Notwithstanding" says Garcillazo (Vol I. page 299) the city contained upwards of 100,000 people of different nations, each might with ease be distinguished "by the colour of the turban, but this mode of distinction was not an invention of the Inca, but a custom of their own." Be this as it may, the manner in which Manco Capac divided the city, is a strong presumptive proof that with him, this also originated. The Temple of the Sun appears to have been a most stately, and magnificent place, and in it, the Spaniards must have found immense riches, the walls being covered with gold, and the Image of the Sun which reached across the east end, was of the same metal, and of great thickness. This Temple is now become the Church of San Domingo. Many of the tombs appear to have been curiously cut out of Crystal, and must have been exceedingly handsome. In some of these repositories, water vases of strange and extraordinary figures, are sometimes found, and I was fortunate enough to alight on two during my stay in Lima. In the immediate neighbourhood of Cuzco there are no rivers, but the small streams are sufficient for the irrigation of the plain. There are but few Spaniards in Cuzco, at present, and I am inclined to believe the natives are anxious to throw off the grievous yoke which they have so long worn. In their stature, the Indians are of a middle height, and muscular, having very little beard, but not as some historians assert, entirely without it; they are of a bright copper colour, wide countenances, without much expreſſion, black eyes, hair of the same colour, which is coarse and long.

Arequipa may be considered the next place of importance, and its extent conceived from the population exceeding 100,000 people who when we were at Lima, were in an open state of rebellion against the State of Spain. The misti, or volcano of Arequipa is one of the highest mountains of the Andes. The section which I here introduce, was taken by Mr. Curson, a gentleman of great knowledge, when he succeeded in reaching the summit, and as it may not have come before the reader already, I hope he will not be displeased by my laying it before him, and when he has given it an examination, he will find that the ſhip being ready for sea, we weighed anchor on the 22d of January, and after a voyage of 20 days, arrived at Juan Fernandez, and notwithstanding we did not find it that earthly paradise described by Lord Anson, it is exceedingly beautiful, and capable of every improvement.

This Island rendered of so much celebrity by the ingenious pen of Daniel De Foe, in his interesting History of Robinson Crusoe, is now become the place of exile for the Patriots of Chili, and it is no more than probable; the suffering of these poor old men will at some

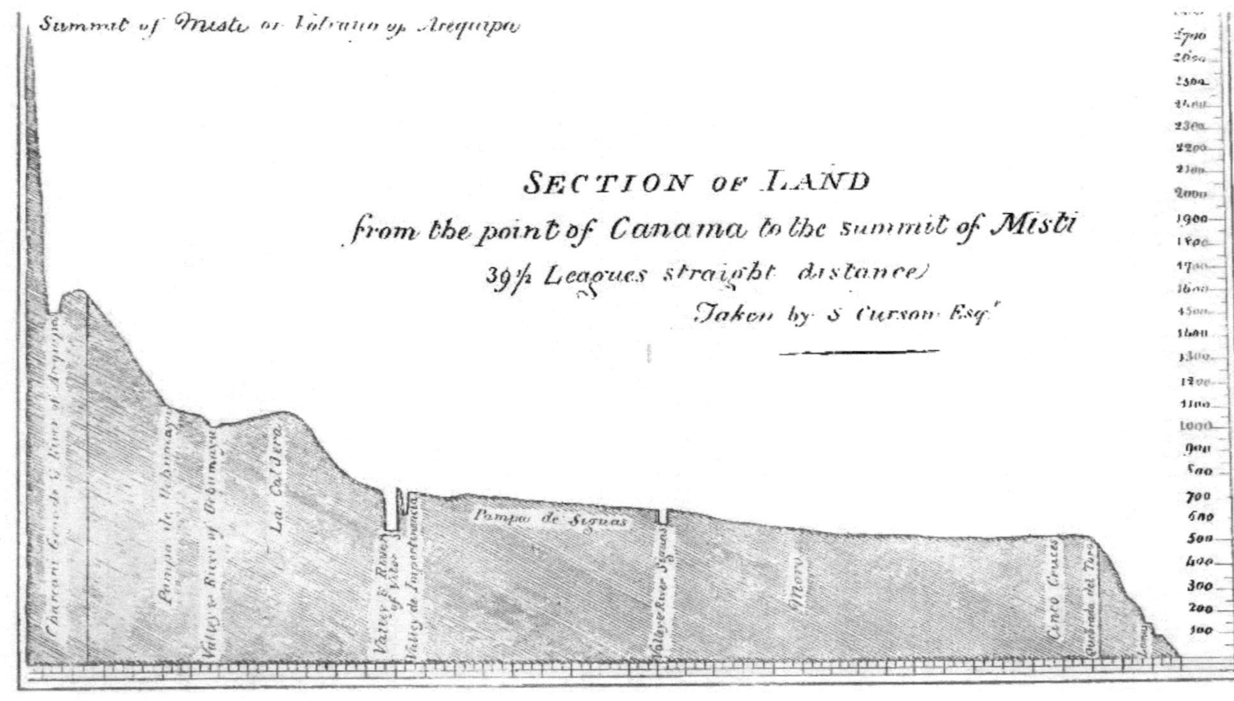
Summit of Misti or Volcano of Arequipa
SECTION OF LAND
from the point of Canama to the summit of Misti
39½ Leagues straight distance
Taken by S Curson Esqr
Charcani Grande & River of Arequipa
Pampa de Uchumaya
Valley & River of Uchumayu
La Caldera
Valley & River of Vitor
Valley de Impertinencia
Pampa de Siguas
Valley & River Siguas
Moro
Cinco Cruces
Quebrada del Toro
Loma

period, prove a theme for another novel of equal interest.

On Ossorio's getting possession of Chili, the head of every family (let his innocence be never so conspicuous) if suspected of being at all hostile to the royal cause, was arrested, dragged from the bosom of his family and friends, and banished to this spot; and on our arrival here, we found about sixty hoary headed venerable men, who had ever been accustomed to the luxuries, and magnificence of a palace, reduced to the lowest ebb of misery, and on the very point of starvation; living in hovels scarcely habitable, and deprived of every thing tending to lighten the grevious yoke of captivity. But a few months before, we had seen many of them living in the greatest affluence, and had often experienced their hospitality. To one of those unfortunate gentleman, whose name is Rosalles, and who had been formerly a member of the Junta, the indulgence of his daughter accompanying him was allowed. This amiable, and affectionate young lady, immediately on her father's arrest solicited herself the favour, and when it was granted to her, she was deaf to all persuasions having a tendency to weaken the resolution she had come to; and to see the care, and assiduity with which she strove to ameliorate his sufferings—to diſſipate his grief—to render his captivity less poignant, was truly admirable, and may we not hope such a genuine mark of filial affection, will ultimately meet with that reward to which it is so pre-eminently entitled!

The principal anchorage in the Island of Juan Fernandez, is Cumberland bay, which is neither commodious, nor safe. Near beach, amongst the various fruit trees, is built a litlle village, where the unhappy victims of the most cruel, unrelenting, and vindictive tyranny reside. The village is commanded by a small battery containing about 100 soldiers badly armed, and miserably equipped. The whole of Juan Fernandez is exceſſively mountainous, and romantically picturesque; poſſeſſing several crystalline streams of water, and a soil of great fertility. It is ſupposed by many to be a volcanic ſubſtance, but, when I succeeded in gaining the summit of several of the mountains, I could not discern the remains of any old craters or eruptions. The mountains are also considered by some to be richly ſtored with ores, and I think it is not improbable, that this may prove, at some future period, to be the case, for luminous bodies, and meteoric ſubſtances are frequently seen to rise from, as well as to descend into several parts of the Island,

A View in the Island of Juan Fernandez.

and, however simple this may appear, it is a strong indication, that ore of some class or other is in the neighbourhood, insomuch, that whenever a phenomenon of this nature is seen by the Devon or Cornifh miners, they always examine the earth, and their search under these circumftances, is generally attended with success. The same may be a criterion for the Island of Juan Fernandez.

The earth of this Island is in many places of the colour of a bright red ochre,* but not, as is afferted in the Voyage of Lord Anson, equal to or exceeding in brilliancy the colour of vermillion. It is very fine, and when ground with oil is a very good pigment, and answers exceedingly well for drapery.

The seeds left here by Lord Anson, have been every where productive, and the peach, the apricot, and nectarine, with plums, &c. grow spontaneously in the woods, with other trees. There is also an abundance of wild turnips, parsley, oats, and the long grass common to European countries.

In ascending the mountains, it is neceffary to use the greatest care, for the looseness of the soil, gives to the trees so little holding,

* See plate which is printed in the native colour of the earth of this Island.

that with many, the weight of a man would be sufficient to precipitate it down the rocks, and with it, if he be not on his guard, he would himself be hurled. This circumſtance renders an excursion of this kind extremely hazardous, and I doubt not intimidates many from undertaking it, and consequently precludes them the pleasure of contemplating the most romantic, strange, and incomprehensible scenery which can be found in the formation of the universe. The box and myrtle trees are every where conspicuous. In the mountains, there are a great number of goats, but are difficult to be taken. There are also a conſiderable number of wild bullocks. The common pigeon of England, become wild, are found in great abundance. There are no venomous reptiles. At certain periods of the year this Island is viſited by the sea lion, which according to the account of Lord Anson, is so immensely large as to produce several hogsheads of blood, as well as much oil and blubber. They are considered a species of the seal, which are found here at times, in great plenty, but during our stay at the island, I did not see any. The number of dolphins and flying fiſh, we saw in Cumberland bay, is really aſtoniſhing, and of the latter some were taken, measuring twenty-six inches. Fiſh of various other sorts are also very plentiful.

To expedite the completion of our wood and water, a tent was conſtructed on ſhore, and two men were kept there during the night to guard the implements for cutting wood, &c. but the temptation was too great to be withſtood by people having so great a propensity to thieving, as the Spaniards, and on the third night some of the garrison entered with their knives, when the man on watch was obliged to fly, the other who was in his hammock, was cut dreadfully, and thrown over the cliff, but he did not receive much injury by the fall, and his wounds were afterwards healed. The depredators plundered the tent of every thing, and escaped with their booty, ere a boat could reach the shore from the ſhip. The governor appeared to make a great ſearch for the articles ſtolen, but I muſt confess, I entertain some doubts whether he was not acceſſary to the affair, and if so he would only be treading in the ſteps of his predeceſſor, who but a few years before plundered the American ship Topaz. (Capt. Folgier) of even every thing she had on board, reserving for his own ſhare all the valuables, among which was a chronometer, belonging to Capt. Bligh of the Bounty, Adams having made it a preſent to Capt. F. at the time he touched at Pitcairn's Island, and which I am given to underſtand he intended to return to its original poſſeſſor.

The temperature of Juan Fernandez, is exceedingly disagreeable, though not unhealthy, and changes three times a day; in the morning it is a thick fog with rain, in the middle of the day exceedingly warm, and at night the wind is ſtrong, and piercingly cold.

Having completed our wood and water, and relieved the unfortunate exiles to the greatest extent in our power, we left Juan Fernandez, and on the 19th of February, came again to an anchor in the Bay of Valparaiso.

CHAPTER VIII.

Sir Thomas Staines having with great kindness acceded to my application for leave to visit the Capital of Chili, and my paſſport from the governor procured, I set off on my journey, at about four o'clock in the afternoon, and reached Casa Blanca soon after eight. It was necessary to halt here for a little refreſhment, as well as to call on the governor or commandant of the place, whom I found, and I doubt not, pleasantly engaged, with some young ladies, at the Curate's house. They were pretty girls, and treated me with great politeness, but as I was anxious to pursue my route, I could not avail myself of their kind invitation, to spend the evening with them.

As the night had shut in, I could see but little of the place, but on my return I found it a long straggling village, ſituated at the end of a barren plain, at about 12 leagues from the port. The inn, if it will bear so dignified a name, is a mean hovel, and in the room where I supped, there were four small beds, on one of which I reposed for a ſhort period. For my supper I had fowls ſtewed in rice, and pickled fiſh; the former was by no mean an objectionable dish. The wine was new and very bad—the spirits not drinkable. My expences here including the horses and guide, amounted to only a dollar.

About twelve o'clock my guide informed me it was time to prepare for ſtarting, or we ſhould have to travel in the heat of the day, to reach Santiago, which he thought would to me be disagreeable. I did not wait a second call, and we were soon on the road.

The night was dark, and chilly, and I found the *poncho*, used by the natives, of greater service than any great coat I could have had. About day-light we reached the summit of the mountain Zapata, which is very high, and we ascended by a zig-zag road made by O'Higgins, an Irishman, in the time of his presidency in the kingdom of Chili. When the fog cleared away, the country around afforded me a most delightful view; the vallies which are all supplied with water, being perfect gardens, and some, of unequalled sterility, forming a ſtriking contraſt. The mountains are very barren, and the earth from most of them is waſhed away. The vallies are perfectly level, and break from the mountains with great abruptness. In the interior of Chili, I did observe any hills running immediately into the plain.

By nine o'clock, we had reached Cura Cavcé where we were joined by a Spanish Gentleman, and an escort of soldiers, with whom I breakfasted on a stew of various ingredients, boiled eggs and *agua dent*, for which repast both parties (eight in number) paid a half dollar. This really excited my astonishment, and I could not but give the child of our host the other half, who prayed to the Holy Virgin to frank me through life with every blessing.

We now proceeded on our journey to the foot of the second *questa* or mountain, when it became quite clear, and the refreshing breeze which had hitherto accompanied us, having died away, we found the heat so oppressive, that we gladly took shelter at a farm-house in the plain of Poangue, which lay near the road, and where we experienced great hospitality from its inhabitants. A repast of meat and fruit was soon ready for us, as well as some of the best wine I found in the country, and after giving a little indulgence to our appetites, we stretched our saddle cloths, and each according to the custom of the country, wrapped himself in his *poncho*, and retired to rest.

About 3 o'clock our guides were again on the alert, who informed us it was time to pro-

Y

ceed, and in a few minutes we were again on the road.

The mountain of Prado,* which was now before us, is of a prodigious height, and as we had left the main road for a nearer cut, and the country bearing nothing but a dry thorn, it was very disagreeable. Here my companion's horse became tired, but not more so, I believe, than he was himself; however, the first difficulty was soon obviated, for a team belonging to some farmers in the neighbourhood was ſtopped in the king's name by the soldiers, and one of the horses taken out, and I doubt not sold immediately on their arrival at the city. The fatigued horse was not left as an equivalent. This incident gave me a pretty clear conception of the beauties of the Spanish constitution, or rather of the grievous burden under which the poor Chilinans groan.

We croſſed this mountain, whose summit afforded me the most rapturous view it is poſſible for the imagination to conceive, or fancy paint. In an instant, the ſtupendous ridge of the Andes or Cordilleras presented themselves to us, reducing those, which I had before considered inaccessible, to the comparative insignificence of a mole hill. This magnificent

---

* This mountain is called by Vancouver, Praow.

chain of mountains, as is observed by Dr. Robertson, no less remarkable for extent, than elevation, rises in different places more than one third above the Peak of Teneriffe, the highest land in the ancient hemisphere. The Andes may literally be said to hide their heads in the clouds; the ftorms often roll, and the thunder bursts below their summits, which though exposed to the rays of the sun, in the centre of the torrid zone, are covered with everlasting snows.*

The city of Santiago was also before us, together with a most extensive plain, beautifully interspersed with villages, rivers, and little hills. These rivers are supplied from the snow, which descends from the Andes. The Maypocho, irrigating the country adjacent to the city, the Mayho and Colina at the distance of six or seven leagues N. and S. render in their respective districts similar benefits.

Descended into the plain, it was with great difficulty my companion (notwithftanding the acquisition of a frefh horse) could travel, therefore on reaching a house three leagues from the city, and being wholly inadequate to pursue his journey, I put him to bed. It was

* Robertson's History of South America, Book IV. page 4.

now late in the evening, and not willing to leave him, I tarried also. The general dish for travellers was soon prepared, and after I had eaten heartily, I endeavoured to sleep, but it was a vain attempt, for the fleas attacked me in such numbers, that I was obliged to retreat from the house, and fortunately I discovered a cart with some ſtraw, which being free from these vermin, I slept profoundly until the morning, when I proceeded on to the city, and reached the hospitable mansion of Sen. Dona Camilita Ramenz de Inquerda. Here I found every thing ready for my reception, every thing I could wish, and away from England, I never spent my time so much to my satisfaction.

I must now take a brief view of Santiago and its vicinity. This city named in compliment to St. James, the patron of Spain, is situated in nearly 33° 45′ south latitude, and about four or five leagues to the west of the Cordilleras or Andes, which run from North to South, through the whole of South America. The plain in which it ſtands, is of unequalled fertility, and not of less extent than thirty to thirty-five leagues in circumference, bounded on the east by the Andes, on the west by the mountain of Prado; by the river

Colina on the North, and on the South by the Mayho.

Peter de Baldivia when he conquered this country, finding a considerable village of Indians on the banks of the Maypocho, laid the foundation of St. Jago, on this luxuriant spot, in the year 1541, and following the example of Pizarro, with that of Lima, laid it out in squares of 150 yards each way, with streets about 30 feet wide, running at right angles, and neatly paved with smooth pebble ſtones; and from the conſtant supply of water conducted to each, by means of canals from the river, they might, with a comparatively small portion of trouble, be of unequalled cleanliness. There are few cities poſſeſſing this advantage, and as few whose inhabitants do not appreciate it.

"The streets which run" says Frazier "from east to west, receive their water from the first canals of the river, and those which cross from North to South, from those which run in the middle of the squares, across the gardens and streets, under little bridges from whence it is caused to flow out. "Were it not for that relief" continues he "the gardens would produce nothing for want of rain for eight months in the year, whereas by this means the city affords all the delight of the country in relation to fruit, and herbs; in the day the cool ſhade, and night the sweet scents of the orange flowers, and floridondoes, which perfume the houses."

The houses are spacious and elegant, notwithſtanding they have only a ground floor. Each has a large square court in front, and a garden behind, and some contain many families. The city possesses no fortification, and is open at every point but the East, where stands the mountain of St. Lucia, which might be occupied to great advantage. Near the centre is the Placa Real, or Royal Square, on the west side of which, is the Cathedral (now, rebuilding,) and Biſhop's Palace, the North is occupied by the Palace of the President, the royal court, council house, and prison. Of these, the two first are handsome buildings. On the east is the market, and a beggarly row of empty shops, and what they call a row of handsome porticos from the South, but the shops under these porticos are very respectable. There is also a gallery on this side, for the purpose of viewing the *torns* or bull fights, which are occasionally exhibited here. In the middle of this square, ſtands a fountain of brass, and I dare say was once as handsome as many writers have described it, but its present appearance does not justify me in drawing any such conclusion.

The market I attended regularly, and found it well supplied with every article of subſistence, and meat much superior to what I expected. The custom-house, and exchange, are superior buildings, but the mint in point of elegance, eclipses any other I saw in South America. Its interior is laid out to greater advantage than that at Lima, though the machinery with which it is worked is nearly the same. The governor of this place, as I have already said of Lima, can order the execution of any man within his goverment, without consulting with, or having the approbation of the President. He is absolute monarch within his walls.

There are many churches here, handsome alone from the quantity of gilding about the various altars, neither of which can be compared, for beauty or elegance, to those at Lima. Here like all other places, where bigotry and superſtition are predominant features, they tell you marvellous ſtories relative to their different images or saints. That one was seen to shed tears of blood—another to kneel—a third to wave its hand at the approach of a profane person; and they believe or fain to believe every thing they relate. However, the seed of luxury, and consequently contempt, which is rapidly disseminating itself in the church, could easily be perceived, for those votaries of idolatry, who but a few years ago thought it sacrilege to prostrate themselves before the altars of their Tutelar Saints, but upon bare stones, have now servants to attend them with soft velvet cushions, which has more the appearance of repose than devotion. To the box, even of the father confeſſor, these articles are also taken.

This city possesses several monaſteries, both for men and women, but they are neither spacious, nor handsome, and resemble those of Lima only in the conduct of their inmates; for, I was assured from the most respectable authority, that the monks, as well as nuns, live the most profligate and licentious lives it is poſſible to conceive, and notwithſtanding they appear to carry under their cloaks or veils, the most rigid religion, when in their cloiſters they throw off their pious maſks, and give themselves up to the illicit enjoyment of those paſſions, which, from their oaths, they are not only bound to deteċt in others, but renounce themselves. This I am fully authorised to say, for I have now in my poſſeſſion the most irrefragable proofs of their guilt; but, says

Dr. Robertson when speaking of the priests, " the giddy, the profligate, the avaricious, to whom the rigid discipline of a convent is intolerable, confider a miffion to America, as a relief from mortification and bondage. There they soon obtain some parochial charge; and, by their situation far removed from the inspection of their monaftic superiors, and exempt, by their character, from the jurisdiction of their diocesan, they are hardly subject to control. According to the teftimony of the most zealous catholics, many of the regular clergy in the Spanish settlements, are not only destitute of the virtues becoming their profeffion, but regardless of that external decorum and respect, for the opinion of mankind, which preserve a semblance of worth, where the reality is wanting. Secure of impunity, some regulars, in contempt of their vow of poverty, engage openly in commerce, and are so rapaciously eager in amassing wealth, that they become the most grievous oppressors of the Indians, whom it is their duty to have protećted. Others with no less flagrant violation of their vow of chastity, indulge with little disguise in the most dissolute licentiousness"

The river Maypocho is in every part fordable, excepting in the rainy season, or when the snow on the mountains melts the most, when it increases to so enormous a degree, that it has been

Z

necessary to build a wall on its left bank, to prevent any injury being done by its great overflow. Its course is very rapid. This wall is perpendicular on each side, about ten feet high, with numerous flights of steps leading to the top, where there is only sufficient room for two or three people to walk conveniently abreast each other. The trees on the inside form a very pleasant shelter from the oppressive rays of the sun throughout ths day. It is called the *Tacamar*, which literally means, to bind or keep back the sea. During two hours of the evening, it is the fashionable resort of the Belles and Beaux of the city, and had it been well arranged at first, it would unquestionably have been the most delightful promenade in that country. Two parties cannot meet, without the one greatly inconveniencing the other, and as there is no walk so pleasing to the fair, this must constantly occur. The bridge which crosses the Maypocho, has eight arches, is well built, and handsome.

During the time of the Patri, or revolution, several wise institutions took place, and to every art or science the greatest encouragement was given, the whole of which, without reserve, was destroyed immediately on the return of the Spaniards to power ; and this extensive city cannot now boast of a school or seminary calculated to expand the mind or enlighten the understanding; neither does any one dare to keep a book, or read one, under a heavy penalty, which has not been approved of by the inquisitor fiscal, or one of his satellites; and even the Bibles and Testaments from the Bible Society, which were promulgated with so much assiduity by Capt. Hellier, were, immediately after his departure, collected by order of the bishop, and publicly burnt.

The inhabitants are voluptuous and indolent, possessing good natural abilities, if properly cultivated. The women, who are generally the best informed, study to rival each other in the personal accomplishments of their children, without paying the least attention to a single mental one; and if their darling boy can strut with grace—adjust his cocked hat—gamble—waltz, and dance a minuet,—it is matter of little consequence, if he knows not the Andes from the Alps; and at maturity he becomes, like his father, too lazy to improve his mind; and too proud and ignorant to allow another to be a superior genius to himself. To this alone can they attribute the loss of that liberty, of which for three years, they were the entire possessors. The women are pretty, interesting, and docile; the men proud, vindictive, revengeful. The character of the Spaniard is inherent in them, except his duplicity, in which they are making rapid strides to attain.

The fashionable hour for visiting, is from ten to twelve at night. They amuse themselves at cards or dancing until a late hour, when they return, make a hasty supper, go immediately to bed, and if they are up a couple of hours before dinner, it may be considered a wonderful exertion. They retire again from three, until six or seven, and after a short walk on the Tacamar, and a little refreshment of preserves, lemonade, &c. &c. they again prepare to visit—some the Tertulia,* others their friends, and many to fly into the arms of their lovers, who are, perhaps, waiting with anxiety at the secret place of assignation. Thus it is, then, their days and nights roll away, and I am persuaded there are few who, possessing enough to satiate their vanity or lust to-day, calculate on the approach of to-morrow. The women, when young, dress elegantly; but at a more advanced age they become such huge monsters, or rather lumps of fat, that any thing elegant loses its effect the instant it is applied; to this there are but few exceptions.

The population of Santiago does not exceed, I

* A gambling-house.

suppose, 50,000 souls, although it is computed to be considerably more. There are a great many slaves, and they are treated with great humanity.

The country, extending towards the River Maypo, Colina and Cordillera Mountains, is particularly beautiful and of uncommon fertility. It is almost a continuation of *cuintus*, or country seats belonging to gentlemen of the city, to which they make frequent excursions, or occasionally retire, as may be most suited to their convenience or taste.

There is a road of communication across the Cordilleras, between Santiago and Buenos Ayres, but for four months it is shut up by the frost, and is at all times difficult to pass. I was given to understand, unless the mules, as well as guides, are experienced, it is exceedingly dangerous, the precipices and chasms being of such stupendous height or depth. Mendoça is the first town you arrive at on the eastern side, when it is a continual plain to the River de la Plata.

The few towns, worthy of notice in the country of Chili, are Valparaiso Penco, or Conception, Cossiepo, Coquimbo, Chilan Quillo, Aconcaqua, Rancaqua Mablie, St. John de la Cordilleria, and Mendoça. The latter being now in possession of the patriots, as well as on the east side of the Cordilleras, I think, ought no longer to be numbered among the cities of Chili. These towns are not very populous, and principally of Mestizoes, Mulattoes, and Indians.

The governor of this kingdom is styled the President, but acts in subordination to the Viceroy of Lima; however, from the remoteness of the situation, as well as not having a convenient communication with that city, it may be said he is quite independent. The residence is always at Santiago, where he is at the head of a court, consisting of four judges, two attorney-generals, with others of subordinate rank, such as reporters, secretaries, &c. &c.

During my visit at this city, an order arrived for the re-establishment of the tribunal of Inquisition, and which was to be put in force at an early period. This court is subordinate to the Limanan one, which sends to Santiago a commissary general, with a necessary number of officers, who are distributed at the different towns, where "they employ themselves," says Frazier, "upon matters of sorcerers true or false, and certain crimes, the cognizance whereof belongs to the Inquisition, as polygamy, &c. As for heretics, I am sure none fall into their hands. They there study so little, that they are not subject to run astray through too much curiosity; only the desire to distinguish themselves from others by an honourable title, make some churchmen learn a little school divinity and morality, to bear the name of a Licentiate, or Doctor, which the Dominicans and the Jesuits confer by a privilege obtained from the Pope, though there is no university established at Santiago; but these titles are to be had of them so easily, that there are some among the licentiates who know little Latin, which they do not look upon as necessary for attaining the sciences."

Whether this writer's observations be just or not, I shall not pretend to determine; but I can say, that on its being made public, that this merciless court was again restored to its original functions, it diffused a general gloom on the countenance of every individual, of whatever class or society. I heard no remark made on the subject; it was prudent perhaps to be silent.

Earthquakes, or *tremblor de tierres*, are frequently felt throughout Chili, and often very alarming; in fact, the city, as well as the other towns, bear evident proofs of it in the structure of their houses; for they are seldom built of a second story, and always with materials well calculated to withstand a sudden shock—such as long unburnt bricks, inlaid with cane, or other stuff of equal elasticity. Among those which have happened here, the most severe was in 1647, when nearly the whole city was destroyed, as well as the greater part of the inhabitants, for those who were not swallowed up in the vortex of this convulſion of nature, became victims to the disease which followed; as the air was, for a considerable period, contaminated by exhalations the moſt unwholesome. Historians say "The earth continued to tremble for three ſucceſſive days". I felt the ſhock of one only, and it was very inconsiderable.

The country throughout, is very rich in ores of every description, particularly gold, silver, and copper, but neither of the mines are now worked to any extent, from the internal commotions, and various revolutions the country has undergone, during these last four or five years. I did not go to the mines, and as there was not a single mineralogist in the country, I was not so successful in procuring specimens as at Lima.

It was but a few days after my arrival at St. Jago, that a report was in circulation of ships of war being seen off Conception, which was followed by the news of the Engliſh squadron having left the port of Valparaiso, in pursuit of them. My feelings, at being left behind, can be with greater ease conceived than describ-ed, for though I was in a house where every thing was at my disposal, I could not but regret being absent, when my presence might have been useful; however, these men of war proved to be clouds, and in a fortnight, the Briton and squadron had returned, when I, wiſhing to secure a paſſage to England, ordered my guide to prepare the horses for ſtarting, and after a journey similar to the one I described in the beginning of this chapter, I arrived on board, where I found, to my great satisfaction, my old friends as I left them, all well, and with me anxious to redouble Cape Horn, and return to that happy country, which poſſeſſed the different objects of our affection, and whose worth could only be appreciated in so remote a region.

CONCLUSION.

The morning of the 28th of March, when we quitted the port of Valparaiso, was of unequalled serenity, but the wind soon veered round to the southward, and occasioned us again to make the Island of Juan Fernandez. Here the breeze became propitious, and as we increased our southern latitude, so did it increase in ſtrength, and on the 13th April we were in the latitude of Cape Horn. The weather had now become tempeſtuous, and the sea rolled from the pole in heavy waves, which roared as they daſhed themselves against the inhospitable ſhores of Terra del Fuego, and Statten Island, but, notwithſtanding this, and our ignorance of the entrance of the ſtraights Le Maire, it was the intention of Sir Thomas to regain the Atlantic by that passage. The fog which had hovered over the land, clearing away, we discovered ourselves a little to the eastward of the entrance, and it was with difficulty we could gain it without being carried by the current upon Statten Island, whose shores bore a moſt terrific appearance. Scarcely had we weathered the rock, and opened the ſtraights, when a sudden guſt of wind carried away the main-yard in the ſlings; but the point was very fortunately gained, and we were soon wafted through into the great Atlantic Ocean, when the carpenters were set to work on the main-yard, and on the fourth day the *fish* was compleated, and it was again aloft. The Tagus, our consort, not being able to follow us through the ſtraights, bore up, and went to the eastward of Statten Island. Nor did she join us again until the 27th of April, when we arrived off the harbour of Rio de Janeiro. In this port we found Admiral Dixon with his squadron preparing to sail for England; our refit was expedited as much as poſſible, and on the 14th of May, we all weighed anchor for our return to this country. During our tedious voyage back, we were first informed of Napoleon's return from Elba to France, which, was ſoon followed by an account of his disaſters at the memorable battle of Waterloo, but we were not put in poſſeſſion of the particulars until the 7th of July 1815, which period brought His Majeſty's ſhip Briton, in safety at Plymouth, and consequently me, to the conclusion of my narrative.

Finis.

J. W. MARRIOTT, Printer, East-Street, Taunton.

DIRECTIONS TO THE BINDER.

N. B. There are in the whole 16 Etchings instead of 18, as mentioned in the Title Page.

ERRATA.

Page	Line	for	Read.
8	2	intered	entered
10	29	unconsionable	unconscionable
13	28	gentleman's	gentlemen's
16	12	to a punishment	to punishment
25	2	is	it
27	21	he dedicated a temple	he dedicated to, &c
37	5	seen	saw
65	10	thought.	intention
—	28	spontaneous.	spontaneously
73	18	bid	bade
79	22	for and carry, &c.	and carry, &c.
99	12	ships—port	shops—part
—	13	affair	affairs
101	28	exhanced.	enhanced
105	1	office	officer
110	9	his	its
111	3	dispatched	dissipated
123	28	contain.	contained
135	22	sticking up before the shoulder, &c.	sticking up, &c.
138	29	not all.	not at all
163	18	Mayho	Maypo
—	12	Ramenz	Ramerez
172	6	hasty.	hearty
173	26	Cossiepo, Quillo,	Copiapo—Quillota—

Zeitfracht Medien GmbH
Ferdinand-Jühlke-Straße 7
99095 Erfurt, Deutschland
produktsicherheit@kolibri360.de